Gre7g Luterman

Skeleton Crew

Special Thanks

To my editor, Kate Blake. Your patience astounds me!
You've been amazing to work with.

To my reviewers: Celia McKechnie, H. Kyoht Luterman,
Ken Barnes, Kyle Banks, Jim Wilbourne, and Denton Warn.
Your critiques helped me see the forest instead of the trees.
Your encouragement kept me going.

To H. Kyoht Luterman for drawing my cover and a
character sheet for the geroo.

To Brandon Kruse for illustrating and inspiring the
design of the White Flower II.

And to Rick Griffin for not only contributing artwork,
and writing _Ten Thousand Miles Up_, but for letting me
play in his universe. It's been great fun tossing Ateri, Jakari,
and the White Flower II into my own adventure.

Links

Aim Ren (interior artwork) http://www.aimren.com

Annie Meneses (interior artwork)
http://www.RoyalSharkArt.com

Brandon Kruse (interior artwork)
http://brandonkruse.tumblr.com/
http://tinyurl.com/mrr78zt

Clockworkpriest (interior artwork)
http://clockworkpriest.tumblr.com

Cunningfox (interior artwork)
http://HollyHindleArt.weebly.com

Gre7g Luterman (story) http://gre7g.com

Goat (interior artwork) http://sketchygoat.tumblr.com

H. Kyoht Luterman (cover & interior artwork)
http://kyoht.com

Kate Watts (editing) http://kateedits.com

Lendsi A. (interior artwork) http://catacujo.tumblr.com

Rick Griffin (world design, interior artwork, and epilogue)
http://housepetscomic.com
http://smashwords.com/profile/view/rickgriffin

Shane Mercer (interior artwork) http://shanemercerart.com

Vanessa P. (interior artwork)
http://plankhandles.tumblr.com/tagged/art

For Kyoht

Anne —
Thank you for helping make
this second edition happen,
I hope you enjoy the tale.

—Greg

Part I
Chapter 1: Sixty Years

"Will it ... hurt?" Sep'ho asked.

He had paid the company administrator little notice, but the question was a welcome distraction from the large, orange pill in Sep'ho's paw.

"Not at all, sir." The administrator tilted his head at Sep'ho's mate in a supportive way, but she ignored him.

The raucous party dropped to hushed whispers, and soon everyone fell silent. All the guests watched as Sep'ho rolled the pill back and forth between his light-colored pads. His heart beat so loudly that he wondered if everyone could hear the blood pounding in his large, pointed ears.

"Thank you so much," Thasha blurted suddenly over the hallowed silence.

Sep'ho turned to face the Happy Couple. She was such a pretty, young thing: skinny, curvy, and covered in beautiful, red fur that puffed on her cheeks. She was so excited that she practically vibrated in place. Both of Thasha's paws clenched her mate's upper arm to her cheek.

Her mate stood at least a head taller than Thasha. His light brown fur stuck up here and there. Sep'ho recognized the dazed expression in his pale, grey eyes. He looked as if he hadn't slept much in the three days since hearing the news.

"Grampa?"

Sep'ho smiled down at his youngest grandson and tousled the cream-colored fur on his head. He borrowed the cub's mug of punch and washed the pill down.

Everyone cheered in unison, "Hooray!"

Sep'ho made a sour face and turned to admonish his daughter. "How much sugar did you put in this stuff? You're never going to get your cubs to bed tonight."

She put her paw to her father's cheek. "It's your special day. They can stay up if they like."

Sep'ho took his strand from the holster on his upper arm and entered a few commands on the display screen. He tapped it against Thasha's, wirelessly transferring his own birth token from one device to the other. He wished the Happy Couple, congratulations.

"Thank you. Thank you so much," Thasha's mate stammered, putting out his paw.

The old male touched the young male's pads with his own. "Good luck." Sep'ho gave him an encouraging smile as he thought back to the day - so many years ago - when he and his mate had become a Happy Couple. Parenthood had been the most exciting - and most terrifying - adventure that the two had shared.

"Good journey!" everyone cheered in unison.

Sep'ho spread his ears in a large, geroo smile as he set his strand on the table. He had enjoyed the party. It had been all that he could have asked for. He raised his voice so that everyone in the crowded, humble apartment could hear. "My mate and I would like to thank you all for coming. Please stay as long as you like - and take some leftovers home with you. Oh, and a special thanks to my son for catering the best meal that I think I've ever had." With a grin, he continued, "I suspect that the captain will be disappointed that he missed it."

The crowd yarped a laugh quietly at the implication, as if the captain regularly attended the Going-Away parties of geroo in Sep'ho's class.

Sep'ho drew a deep breath with eyes closed, savoring all the familiar smells of friends, family, and the apartment he shared with his mate. He felt paws carefully removing his finest choker of glass beads, the faux-leather strand holster on his arm, and the silver bracelet he wore around the base of his tail.

Sep'ho smiled at his daughter as she replaced his adornments with festively colored crepe. "You look very handsome, Dad," she assured him.

Sep'ho's family and the Happy Couple walked him through the front door and out into the corridor. "Sixty years," he reminisced quietly to himself. "How quickly it's gone. ..."

A year was a meaningless measure here in the depths of space. No one aboard had ever set paw on Gerootec, and none would ever return to it. It hardly mattered how long it took the lush, green ball to orbit its star. The geroo had kept the convention of measuring time in years, but they had simplified them by dropping leap days and other such adjustments that would keep measured time in sync with the seasons.

He put his arm around his mate's shoulders, and she buried her muzzle into the side of his neck, wetting his salt-and-pepper fur with tears. They had no words. Everything had been said.

The old geroo led the party down the corridor. Others, sensing the occasion, made way for the group. They headed down the deck, toward the center of the ship. His greying paws padded silently past rows of other working class apartments.

Working class was a bit of a misnomer aboard the White Flower II. Everyone worked. From the moment cubs were old enough to go to school until they had used up their allotment of years, everyone worked. Although a crew of ten thousand seemed large, the generation ship was a city unto itself. Everyone had to pull his or her fair share. No one was allowed to shirk that responsibility.

No one was allowed to waste away from old age.

The crew wished they could have more time, of course, but everyone understood – school drilled it into them from a very young age – that the ship could only support ten thousand souls. If the company allowed more to be born (or wasted resources caring for those who could no longer contribute), it would surely lead to the death of them all.

No, all the crew had to make the best of their sixty years, and those young couples who wanted to conceive had to wait for an opening, just as Thasha and her mate had waited for Sep'ho's time to come to an end.

Sep'ho took a bad step and stumbled, but his mate and son caught him before he could fall. The old geroo giggled a bit. The weight of his daily concerns had lifted from his shoulders. He felt a little light-headed.

"Let me help you, Pop," his son said. He put his father's arm around his shoulders.

They walked on through the busy market. Many recognized the kindly old geroo and waved to him as he passed. "Good journey!" "Good journey, Sep'ho!" "Good journey!"

"Don't cry," he whispered to his mate, "don't be sad."

His feet wouldn't cooperate, but it didn't matter. He floated through the air, supported easily on all sides by the six who cared for him most. He stretched back, flat, and stared into his mate's brown eyes. Loose ends of yellow crepe fluttered behind him. "I love you," he whispered.

"I love you, too," she said through the tears. But Sep'ho's blue eyes stared off at nothing, unfocused.

A young male carrying a stack of boxes set his load down in the corridor and rushed to help. He took Thasha's place.

"Good journey," she whispered before she turned away, "and thank you."

Others did the same – friends and strangers alike. They all took turns carrying Sep'ho's body on to its final destination. The corpse traveled on a conveyor belt of paws: some helping to carry him for only a few meters and some much farther before they returned to their duties.

Sep'ho's body left the market, and then down, down the long and winding ramp to the very bottom of the ship. Here in the bowels of the White Flower II, the air was a little too stale, a little too warm, a little too humid. The lights high overhead shone a little more dimly here; the inhabitants looked a little more shabby. But even down here, the geroo passing by were quick to help take up a share of the burden. They all wished him *good journey*.

At long last, six strangers carried the body to a wide, steel door marked with flashing lights and yellow caution lines. Six strong workers with grime-encrusted fur stood waiting for Sep'ho to arrive.

The tallest geroo spoke up. "Thank you all," she said. "We'll take him from here."

Carefully, respectfully, the waiting workers took over the procession, swapping places with the geroo who delivered the body. After a brief pause, Kanti, a young male with shaggy, tan fur, punched his access code into the phone on his arm.

The six waited patiently with their burden as the four sections of the gigantic door creaked and groaned, ever so slowly retracting back into the walls to reveal the immense space – and pungent aroma – of Recycler Bay Two.

Kanti put his pads on the old geroo's chest for a moment, and looked into his unseeing eyes. "Farewell, sir. Good journey."

"Good journey," the other five whispered in unison before setting off once more on the short walk to the recycler.

Eye color commonly ranges from gold to brown. Blue and green are less common.

K·14

Species: Geroo

Fur ranges in color; anywhere from white, grey, and black, to tans, browns, reds, and golds. Pelt markings vary from individual to individual with solids, spots and agouti being the most common.

Nose and paw pads range from pink to tan.

Blunt claws used for social grooming.

Square, human-like teeth inside of mouth, except for large, pointed canines.

Tail may be ringed, solid, or tipped in either light or dark fur.

Bottom side of right foot.

Chapter 2: Extra Shifts

The six walked down the blue, no-skid deck, past sorted heaps of refuse to the long, constantly moving conveyor that kept the recycler fed. Normally piled with a careful mix of trash, the conveyor emptied while the workers waited to receive the body. Recycling corpses on an empty conveyor was the best the crew could do – under the circumstances – to preserve the deceased's dignity.

They laid him to rest gently on the center of the belt with his head pointed toward the deep, violet glow. Kanti took a moment to cross the old male's arms across his chest and straighten his short legs to either side of his broad tail. Then Kanti adjusted the yellow crepe so that it wouldn't look haphazard. Admittedly an unnecessary gesture, it made him feel better to see the dead sent off in a respectable manner. It lessened the loss, somehow, that he felt for his own parents.

Kanti stepped back beside the belt with his five coworkers and waited in silence as violet light and a deep, bass hum slowly swallowed the body.

Out of their sight, the corpse drifted weightlessly into the belly of the beast. The recycler released the bonds between the corpse's atoms, and they drifted gently into a gaseous form.

The recycler was one leg of "the trinity": three advanced krakun technologies that made life aboard a generation ship like the White Flower II possible. With an indeterminately long mission, all waste matter aboard the ship had to be recycled. The ship's only loss of mass over the centuries was from fuel conversion of matter to energy.

After reducing matter to constituent atoms, the recycler spun the output in a series of zero-g vortexes to sort the atoms by mass. It routed different elements to a hundred different chambers and then rebonded them into molecules. The recycler coalesced metals into ingots that would then be used in the on-board factories. It reassembled some simple molecules to form fresh air, clean water, and various other essentials.

The krakun didn't design the recycler to form complex structures. One couldn't program it with a description of Chocolate Delight, for instance. But it did generate a steady supply of vitae – a green, gooey mix of simple nutrients used to fertilize the geroo's crops. It produced the liquid hydrogen that fueled the vehicles that harvested the grain. Waste heat from the recycler powered the ovens aboard the ship. Anything the crew manufactured drew from these recycled resources or from other products that could be traced back similarly.

Having done their part, the six returned to their duties. They boarded bright green bulldozers and began to push loads of refuse back onto the belt.

Taskmaster - a display screen in the cab of each vehicle - kept the operators constantly informed on the balance of the mix. Kanti's blazed red with a plea for more organics. He made a foul face at the thought. The ship's plumbing pumped sewage directly into the recycler, thankfully, but the ship's garbage chutes piled food waste into wet, stinking mounds. No one liked being assigned to get organics.

With a resolved sigh, Kanti drove off to a far corner of the bay, looking for a heap that he hoped was dry enough not to splash up into the bulldozer's cab.

§

After a few hours of loading organics, Kanti's screen blinked blue. The scruffy geroo smiled and drove the dozer back to the blue deck of the fueling area, where the next shift of workers gathered to take over.

"Kanti!" a voice shouted as he walked toward the bay doors. "Wait up!"

Kanti's best friend, Saina, jogged over from his bulldozer. He stopped beside Kanti, doubled over, and struggled to catch his breath. His broad tail hung straight down, tapering to a narrow tip just above the tops of his heavy work boots.

"You're really out of shape," Kanti teased.

"No," Saina wheezed, "I was never ... 'in shape'." Saina was roughly the same height and color as his scruffy friend, but instead of having Kanti's lean and lanky build, Saina was round and carried most of his weight in a wide belly that sagged down in front of him.

"Boys! I'm glad I caught you."

Kanti turned about to find himself face-to-chest with his supervisor, Tish.

At 190cm in height, Tish was as tall as a support column and about as shapely. She wasn't an ugly female, but neither was she particularly feminine.

Adolescent males spent their nights dreaming of short, round females with more scent than muscle. But between an unlucky draw from the genetic lottery and the recycler bay's stench masking all personal scents, Tish was destined to be just "one of the guys" among her workmates.

It really didn't help that she acted like one of the guys too. Kanti forgot she was female on more than one occasion, and he knew he wasn't alone in this. At least *he* had never accidentally called her "sir."

"Do you guys know Ghaddi?" Kanti and Saina both shook their heads. "He works second shift. Flipped his dozer last night. Busted himself up pretty badly."

Kanti's triangular ears drooped in concern. His fleshy, chevron nose twitched. "Is he going to be okay?"

Tish punched him cordially in the shoulder. "Nothing they'll recycle him over," she yarped a laugh. "But he can't operate a dozer for a while. Not until he's off the pain meds, at least.

"Second shift was already short-staffed, and it's never going to make quota with only four guys. We put in a request for some temporary help, but even if we got a replacement tomorrow, we'd still need to train them." Tish sighed and put her fists on her narrow, masculine hips. "If you could help out, I've got an authorization for overtime …"

"I guess I could take a shift on the sixth," Kanti said without enthusiasm. "It was supposed to be my day off."

"Thanks, Saina," she said, flubbing Kanti's name. She turned to Saina. "How about you, Kanti?"

Saina started to shake his head, but Kanti flashed his teeth and gave him a warning stare with his piercing, green eyes, cowing him.

"Yeah, okay."

Saina didn't look happy, but Tish failed to notice. "Thanks, guys!" she shouted over her shoulder as she raced off to try to catch some other departing workers.

"What's the big idea?" Saina whined. "I don't *do* overtime."

Kanti glared icily at him. "It was your stupid idea not to correct her when she got the two of us mixed up."

"It was my *hilarious* idea," Saina corrected him.

"It was funny," Kanti agreed, "at first. But she's been our supervisor for almost a year now. How much longer is this gonna' go on?"

Saina shrugged apathetically. "I've got lots of years left."

"And what happens when she logs that *Saina* volunteers to take extra shifts, but *Kanti* is a slacker?" He snatched the communicator off of his shoulder and waved it in his buddy's face. "Besides, if my overtime pay ends up in your strand, then you better earn at least as much overtime for mine."

Kanti stared at his friend for a good, long moment. "So do you want me to keep playing along, or not?"

"Okay. Okay," Saina conceded. He put his arm around Kanti's shoulders. "Whatever you say. Just don't spoil the fun ... yet."

KANTI SAINA TISH

Chapter 3: The Pill Bottle

The richest geroo lived at the top of the ship, with the fanciest apartments and nicest shops. Kanti had never seen the insides of any of those apartments, but he had heard the rumors of their enormous size and luxurious amenities. Could those rumors really be true? Was it even possible that only a few, privileged geroo claimed entire decks of the ship?

The poor lived in crowded conditions at the bottom of the ship – level twenty-five. The extra-tall deck housed a general mess hall and a barracks-style dormitory. No one paid to use either, so they acted as a safety net for hapless geroo. No matter how far down on their luck, the crew could always count on a hot meal and a dry place to sleep in the belly of the White Flower II.

Kanti ate in the free mess once or twice a week to save money, but he had his own apartment on twenty-four. It was a dreary, dreadful place, but at least it was private. As much as he hated blowing half of his pay on rent, he wasn't ready to give up the apartment.

Kanti and Saina headed up a few decks. Most decks were arranged around an open market, but the one on twenty-five wasn't known for food or drink. Even the cheapest food could not compete with the mess hall.

Saina gestured at a vendor with two fingers. She poured a pitcher of dark orange wine into two plastic cups and bumped her strand against his to complete the transaction.

Kanti thanked his best friend for buying the first round and took a gulp from his cup. The wine was sweet and weak; bitter, but not unpleasantly so.

Strictly speaking, all krakun vessels prohibited alcohol. But enforcement of that law was half-hearted at best. Showing up to work drunk might land a crewman before a judge, but only the krakun really cared if anyone drank during their down-time.

If a krakun caught someone drinking, he'd probably toss that geroo in the recycler. But that's how the monstrous creatures handled most problems they encountered. Fortunately, the White Flower II seldom hosted anyone from Krakuntec. The commissioner visited periodically to check on the ship, but he wasn't liable to stroll down any of the decks – not any of the ones with a three-meter clearance, at least.

Kanti bought a meat-and-cheese roll. He sat down at a plastic table near the small stage at the center of the market and turned his seat to watch the band play. The company didn't pay anyone to play music, of course. It required everyone to work a job that contributed to the welfare of the mission, but no one cared what the crew did after hours – what geroo did with their pay or how they earned some extra – as long as it didn't hurt anyone else.

The music was pretty decent, for a lower-deck venue, at least. They had a pop sound that wasn't all polished and refined. The band covered a few recent hits, but mostly played original songs with amusing (if slightly risque) lyrics. Kanti didn't bother downloading any of their tracks onto his strand, but he enjoyed listening to them play live. He retrieved their schedule to see when they played next.

Despite the crew's isolation in deep space, krakun ships had a vibrant digital marketplace. Anyone could upload original media to the network and set their own prices for downloads. Whenever the commissioner visited, his ship's computer automatically synced content with the White Flower II's computer, giving the crew access to a digital marketplace that stretched across the galaxy.

Once, when Kanti was an adolescent, his father tried to explain to him how the computers automatically scaled revenues to avoid trade deficits between vessels. His father loved economics and read everything he could find on the subject, but to Kanti the explanation was all just numbers moving around between accounts.

Kanti didn't excel in any of his studies, really. He enjoyed working with his paws, building things or taking them apart. Math confused him, and although he could read, Kanti found it tiresome and boring. Even though the work was far from glamorous, his job at the recycler made him feel good. He could see what needed to be done and appreciated how important it was that someone do it. Completing his quota made him feel accomplished – even if it did involve loading organics that day.

Saina wasn't paying attention to the band. He turned his seat around and leaned over to the pair of females sitting at the next table. Kanti wished he could be more charming and friendly, like his best friend. He'd love to date, but never felt as if he had much to offer a potential mate. What female wanted a male with a low pay-grade job, a coat that smelled of refuse, a dismal apartment, and who couldn't even provide her with offspring? Kanti couldn't imagine why they would.

Besides, he had enough problems, and they'd only get more complicated if he had a mate who wanted him to be something that he couldn't.

Saina stood and offered his paw to one of the females. She took it with only minor hesitation, and they headed out onto the dance floor, in front of the band. Kanti sighed inwardly, but put on a brave face, determined to try and do the same. "Great band, huh?" he said to the lone, remaining female.

The girl looked up from her drink, and their eyes met for a moment. She was cute, he supposed. She had a white pelt with a brown spot that surrounded her left eye. Her ears were petite, and he thought that she might smell nice, but she made a display of sniffing the air when Kanti leaned a little closer to her table.

"What's that ... smell?"

Kanti chuckled nervously. "Yeah, Saina and I both work at the recycler," he explained. "I loaded organics today, and I haven't been back to my apartment yet to clean up. ..."

Her expression soured, and his stomach sank. She mumbled an excuse and left the table before Kanti could even learn her name.

"Nice meeting you," he muttered into his drink with a shrug. Kanti poured the remaining wine down his throat and took one last look over at Saina and his dance partner before heading away from the market.

Kanti didn't want to be a "creased whisker," as the geroo called it. He didn't want to crowd Saina, should the two prefer some privacy.

Premarital sex had been taboo back on Gerootec, but the social mores had shifted over the generations aboard the White Flower II. With krakun technology able to cure all diseases, and keeping the females crew members sterile until they had authorization to reproduce, there was very little downside to promiscuity. Geroo often pair-bonded for life, but the search for that mate evolved into something far more exciting than it had been back on feudal Gerootec.

Kanti headed off to the gravity down-wells and hopped back to deck twenty-four. The wells were essentially stair-wells without the stairs – simple platforms that geroo could jump off to reach the level below. The artificial gravity in the wells was turned down to a tiny fraction of normal, so each hop was slow and gentle.

Each platform shadowed the opening down to the next level; so to travel multiple levels, one simply hopped, turned around, and hopped again until reaching the desired deck. The overlapping structure ensured that a geroo could not fall multiple levels accidentally.

Forward-thinking geroo did all their serious drinking on decks higher than their home deck. Although hopping up levels was no harder (the up-wells used the same fraction of gravity, it was just set to pull in the opposite direction), the transition zones into and out of the up-wells could be pretty hard on crewmen who had had too much to drink.

Kanti didn't envy the janitorial staff when they had to clean vomit out of the wells.

The scruffy geroo walked down the stuffy, poorly lit corridor to a scuffed, non-descript door labeled 2475B. He punched his code into the strand on his shoulder, and the door lock clicked. With a rough shove, he pushed the door open a few centimeters before it struck some object piled up in the doorway beyond.

Kanti rested his head against the door for a moment with his eyes closed and listened to the buzzing of the corridor light as it flickered overhead. He squeezed inside the barely open door and closed it behind him without turning on the light.

He knew it was silly. Not seeing the piles of junk that filled the apartment didn't make it go away, but at least this way he didn't feel the tightening in his throat, the quickening of his pulse, the desire to flee back out into the corridor.

Kanti picked his way carefully down the narrow trail between the stacks of his mother's possessions. Cleaning day was coming. ... He had intended to start dragging her stuff down to the recycler on his day off. Then he sank in on himself, remembering that he agreed to work it. He sighed, "I guess I'll start on it **next** week." He had said that before.

After stubbing his toe once or twice, he reached the hall-way that led to his bedroom. He stopped for a moment at his parents' room, and his paw moved involuntarily to the light switch. Against his better judgment, he turned it on and stared at her bed.

Apart from the additional layer of dust, the scene hadn't changed in two years. The covers were still thrown back. The little wine remaining had evaporated, but the cup sat untouched where it had been left on the nightstand. The empty bottle of his father's painkillers still lay beside it. The sight made him angry, but not as it had before. The feeling had muted somehow, deadened by a heaviness. More than anything, he just felt tired.

Chapter 4: Head-count

Captain Ateri stood in the airlock, waiting for it to finish cycling the air. He held his nose with one paw and popped his ears. The heat and additional pressure was unpleasant, but it was the high sulfur content of krakun air that he really hated. It burned his remaining eye and overwhelmed his sense of smell.

Whenever Commissioner Sarsuk summoned the captain into a meeting, he set the atmosphere in his chamber to a compromise between the air of Krakuntec and that of Gerootec. The experience was unpleasant for both of them, but the ship's medical officer assured Ateri that he should suffer no long-term harm in the exposure to so much sulfur.

Why they couldn't just meet via com-link or at a reasonable hour were other issues entirely.

The bolts cranked open, and the captain swung the heavy door aside. He steadied himself as he stepped onto the painted metal deck. A half-dozen gravity generators focused on the commissioner's chamber, their outputs phased to interfere constructively and destructively.

The engineers assured Ateri that the effect on someone of Sarsuk's size was quite pleasant. The commissioner would feel as if he rested on a cloud, but without all the unpleasantness that came with low-gravity environments. He wouldn't feel as if he were falling and he'd have no difficulty getting traction when he wished to move about. It was a high-tech alternative to loading the chamber with tons and tons of bedding that would be difficult to launder in the confines of a star ship.

For someone of Ateri's height, however, the modified gravity wasn't so wonderful. The standing waves caused vertigo whenever he moved his head and could lead to motion-sickness during a long meeting. He knew that his comfort, however, wasn't one of Sarsuk's concerns.

The captain glanced around the cavernous chamber. Prints of gloomy landscapes (for those who could not see infrared and ultraviolet, at least) adorned the faux-stone walls. "You wanted to see me, sir?"

The commissioner ignored the tiny captain for a while, making him wait – pointlessly – while he tapped the screen on his strand with a long, curved claw. Ateri folded his paws behind his back and waited patiently to be addressed. He craned his neck up to look at the commissioner's massive face, several stories overhead.

"Are you aware," the commissioner began, "of the conviction of Doctor Hitera?"

Ateri nodded. "Of course. Our court is autonomous, but they report all convictions and crew issues to me." He shook his head slightly with regret. "They came down on him with all four paws – a lifetime ban from medicine and a ten-year sentence."

Sarsuk ignored the captain again and read an excerpt of the report out loud. Ateri grabbed his own communicator off of his shoulder and pulled up the report. "The witness, A'jira, twenty-eight, submitted to the court a secret recording of the suspect, Doctor Hitera, forty-five, requesting a sum of ten thousand credits to help her get pregnant – despite his knowledge that an additional birth token had not been obtained."

Ten thousand birth tokens circulated continuously around the ship. The small files, kept on strands, legitimized a geroo's existence. Each crew member held one for life and passed it along to a Happy Couple when his or her time was over.

Ateri nodded somberly as he pretended to read along with the commissioner. He knew that Sarsuk's copy of the report omitted that A'jira tried to negotiate a much lower fee. In his mind, the very fact that she recorded the conversation proved that she tried to blackmail the doctor for bargaining leverage. The doctor must have thought she was bluffing when she was not.

If left up to me, Ateri thought, *I'd have had them both publicly flogged.* He could have kept that from the commissioner entirely, and his crew wouldn't be down a doctor, now.

"How in the names of the dead gods did something like this happen?" Sarsuk roared, making Ateri's teeth rattle.

The captain just shrugged. "Everyone with power must battle with temptation. It is impossible to predict just who will become corrupted. ..."

Sarsuk grunted dismissively. "I don't care if your crew is corrupt!"

Ateri folded his paws and stared blankly up at the commissioner, trying to mask his surprise.

"I don't care if you rule your people with an iron fist or let them vote on every issue. I don't care if you worship the dead gods or the spirits of your ancestors. I don't care if this ship is a crime-free utopia or if you kill each other to get ahead. Your people brought their own laws with them when you came aboard our ship. We didn't tell you how to run your lives."

The krakun, like every civilized race in the galaxy, had laws governing their behavior. But from the commissioner's point of view, the geroo were little more than insects scrabbling in the dirt. What one insect did to another was largely irrelevant to the krakun.

Commissioner Sarsuk leaned slowly down so his warty, sandy yellow face was mere centimeters from the furry geroo. The jagged edges of his polished, white teeth gleamed in the room's purple-tinted light. The commissioner licked his lips with his light blue, triply forked tongue. "Planetary Acquisitions really only cares about the substantial investments they have made in this vessel and the mission. Specifically, that you take good care of our ship, that you research the planets we assign you to investigate, and that you obey the ship's bio-limit of ..." He glanced back to the screen, "Six hundred thousand crew‐years."

Sarsuk ground his teeth together in frustration with a deep bass rumble that set Ateri's fur on end. "If the little vermin are breeding without your control, then the whole vessel will death-spiral right into uninhabitability." A gravelly edge entered the commissioner's voice, causing Ateri's gut to clench. "I will not lose one of my ships because you can't control your crew!"

"Commissioner!" Ateri said, clearing his throat. "The court convicted Doctor Hitera of **conspiracy** to circumvent ship protocol. There's no evidence that he – or that anyone else – has ever helped someone reproduce without a permit, or that he even would've in this case. For all we know, he could have been trying to scam that young lady out of her money without any intention of carrying through. He could have been plotting to surreptitiously divert a legitimate birth token. We don't even know if he **could have** done such a thing without us finding out about ..."

"Enough!" Sarsuk bellowed. The commissioner's cavernous throat was so large that Ateri could have walked down it without ducking.

The word rang in Ateri's sensitive ears. The captain made a show of adjusting the black patch that covered his left eye as he waited for his hearing to return.

"I do not need your could-haves or your should-haves," the enormous creature growled. "There are stowaways aboard my ship."

"Stowaways?"

"Yes, anyone bred without authorization is just as illegitimate as had they snuck on board."

Sarsuk's head hung in front of Ateri for a long while. The rotten-meat stench of the creature's breath could not be ignored, but the captain refused to let it show on his face.

"You will get me a list of everyone over the last fifty years who has had the ability to enable procreation."

"Yes sir." Ateri tapped notes onto his strand.

"You will get me a log of every time that this has been done over the same period."

"Check."

"You will come up with options – ways to keep this from ever happening again."

"Check."

"Ways to detect that it has happened, when your solutions fail me."

Ateri kept his expression neutral. "Check."

"You will take an exact head-count of your crew. You will estimate how badly you have exceeded the White Flower II's bio-load. You will calculate how much compensation will be required, and you will recycle as many of your crew as needed to ensure a rebound." Sarsuk stared at the little geroo with his gigantic, slitted, green eyes. "I don't care if you have to save semen samples of all your males and reduce down to a skeleton crew of breeding-age females. I ... will ... not ... lose ... this ... ship."

"Sir," Ateri swallowed, "we perform a census every year. It has never ... in the entire history of the mission ... showed any deviation from our anticipated head-count."

"Of course it hasn't," Sarsuk replied immediately. "No stowaways would include themselves in your census. You need to count them in a way that cannot be subverted."

"No."

There was a perceptible pause. "No?"

"No, sir," Ateri corrected himself.

"You've defied me twice before," Sarsuk said smoothly. "The first time earned you *a hundred* lashes. The second time cost you your eye. I wouldn't have given any other geroo on board a second chance, and now you're daring to defy me for a third time?

"Do you know why I haven't recycled you ... yet?" The commissioner didn't wait for a reply. "Because it's bad for morale to recycle a ship's captain. Nothing more. You're not special, Ateri. It'd be bad for morale to reduce all your males to frozen, specimen jars, but I will order that too if you push me."

"Sir, you can recycle me if you wish. I'm not refusing an order because I do not wish to carry it out. I am refusing it because I'm incapable of carrying it out."

Sarsuk pulled his head away from the geroo in surprise. The captain was as brash as any. He had never claimed to be incapable ... of anything.

"I don't believe that there are stowaways hiding aboard my ship," Ateri explained, "but if there are, the ship has no internal sensors to detect them, nor to give me a head-count any more precise than a manual census.

"If I wanted to get an infallible head-count, I'd have to move the entire crew to the shuttle deck and then search the rest of the ship for stowaways with only my most loyal offi-cers." He straightened his back and stared straight ahead at the commissioner's taloned feet. "Depressurizing the rest of the ship to clear it might be quick, but it'd cause irreparable harm to our bio-load, so my officers would have to search room-by-room, deck-by-deck - under every bed, behind every panel, inside every access tube. The process would take months ... perhaps even years. The logistics of keeping the crew alive and fed during that time, while no one is working, is simply impossible. I assure you that the ship would be lost if we attempted such madness."

Sarsuk would never admit that he was wrong. Ateri waited in the prolonged silence, wondering if the enormous alien would just crush him and promote someone else to take his place.

"Find another way," the commissioner said at last.

"Yes, sir."

Artwork ©2015 Clockworkpriest

Chapter 5: Insomnia

Kanti checked his strand again. It was still only a little after 0200 hours. He cursed himself for going to bed early. He should have stayed to watch the band. Even if it **had** made Saina uncomfortable for Kanti to sit there alone while Saina was with a date, he should have stayed up.

He closed his eyes again, but they popped back open only moments later.

He wanted to go. More than anything else, he wanted to get out of that forsaken apartment, and go.

Slowly, he dropped his paw off the side of the bed, down on top of the rough canvas bag. ***No, it's a bad idea,*** he thought, ***an addiction that has to be fought.*** He folded his fingers together. But only a couple of moments later, he clutched the bag to his chest.

Of all the many items in the apartment, this was the only one he cared about. Oh sure, he'd be lost without his communicator, but the bag was his escape.

Despite his heavy work boots, he tiptoed through the apartment's detritus with the grace of a dancer and was out to the corridor in moments. He threw the bag across his back and thanked his lucky stars that he had found it discarded in the recycler bay.

The White Flower II was a working ship, but it was also a city. There was a little crime for the security officers to contend with; geroo sometimes did what they shouldn't do, they sometimes went where they shouldn't go. But by and large, the officers trusted the crew. The doors to the drive room were left unlocked, as were the control panel covers, and even the access tube hatches.

When someone opened a hatch, the ship's computer logged an event in engineering. One of the duty officer's chores was to check the logs, and if he noticed that no maintenance was scheduled in the area, then – and only then – would security be notified to search the tubes for mischief-makers. Any crew members who passed by wouldn't even look twice if they saw a geroo climbing into one of the tubes that criss-crossed the ship - especially if that crew member carried an engineer's bag. The Planetary Acquisitions logo - a black, krakun claw gripping a planet over a field of blue - enabled him, encouraged him to explore.

Kanti strolled casually to an access hatch on level twenty. Apart from the occasional maintenance worker, the corridors on twenty tended to be empty at this hour. Only a few of the ship's marketplaces remained open this late, catering to the second and third shift crews. He saw no one tonight.

Exploring restricted portions of the ship was a risky endeavor for any geroo - doubly so for anyone with as much to hide as Kanti. Krakun vessels were renowned for the harshness of their justice.

Kanti sealed the hatch behind him and flipped on his flashlight. He inspected the hatch sensor and made sure the wire he had previously shorted across the terminals was still in place. It was; no alert would be logged tonight. He removed the short and strapped the air monitor to his right shoulder.

Like all of his gear, he had found the air monitor in a heap, waiting to be recycled. The battery had to be replaced, but the unit appeared to function. He tested it by putting it in a plastic bag and breathing the air around it until the carbon dioxide level became hazardous. The alarm was so loud that he dropped it on the deck in surprise.

The tubes weren't all dangerous, but they could be. Pipes of all sorts ran along the tube walls, and any one of them could develop a pinhole leak. Unlike the air in the ship's living areas, the air quality in the tubes went unmonitored, so deadly levels of various gasses could easily build up, unnoticed.

Kanti worked his way through the system of access tubes, shorting out hatch sensors where he could, and changing routes when he could not. Soon he came to a very heavy door labeled with ice crystal and flame warning icons – a bulkhead baffle.

Outer space was the strangest environment the geroo had ever encountered. Although incredibly cold, space was also a great insulator. The baffles between the ship's outer shell and the living spaces inside, could become dangerously hot as well as dangerously cold. And if that didn't make the bulkhead baffles dangerous enough, should a micrometeorite pierce the bulkhead, anyone inside the baffle would surely be killed.

A digital display panel was inset into the hatch. Kanti wiped the dust off of it with his pad; a blue light indicated that it was safe to enter, but the display listed the temperature inside as 37 degrees below freezing. He hesitated for a few moments while he decided whether he dared to adventure farther.

If an engineer had to work inside the baffle, he'd bring protective clothing and an air processor to pre-warm the air he breathed in. Kanti had no such things.

He dug through his bag and found a thick pair of oversized oven mitts molded out of silicone. They wouldn't keep him from freezing, but at least he'd be able to crank open a hatch to get back out. Grabbing -37 C metal with bare pads would cause instant frostbite.

Kanti put the flashlight in his mouth and cranked the hatch open, swinging it wide and exposing the thick foam insulation that lined the inside of the hatch. When the cold air hit him, he gasped so hard that he nearly dropped the flashlight.

Had he done that inside the baffle, it could have been deadly. His heart raced, and he thought about just how close he could have come to dying. He slammed the hatch shut to reconsider.

Geroo were covered with fur, but their fur wasn't thick. It was just warm enough that no one needed clothing within the ship's living spaces. Their fur certainly wasn't sufficient for sub-zero temperatures.

As unhappy as he was with his life, Kanti did not want to die exploring the ship.

He considered returning to his gloomy apartment.

With one last breath of warm air, Kanti swung the hatch open and climbed inside. The cold hit him like a hammer, folding his ears back flat and retracting his testicles tightly up inside his body. He started shivering instantly. He exhaled slightly, and a huge plume of frozen vapor flashed in the bluish flashlight beam.

The baffle was huge – only a meter thick, but perhaps five stories high, and just as wide, though it was difficult to tell for certain. The enormous darkness devoured his flashlight's feeble beam. He stood on a small ledge, a couple of floors up from what he believed to be the bottom of the baffle. Rungs led up, down, and across the great expanse of bulkhead.

Kanti grabbed onto the rungs with his oven mitts and started to climb. He was relieved to find that very little gravity existed here. He must have been just outside the beams of the gravity generators at the bottom of the ship.

With a few quick motions, Kanti pulled himself up to the next closest hatch that he could see. His boots made a strange, hollow, clanging noise each time that they struck metal. It reminded him that only a thin wall of aluminum separated him from hard vacuum and certain death. The strange sound make him feel trapped in a frozen, metal tomb.

Kanti inspected the hatch quickly, but the sensor was on the other side; he had no way to short it out from here. He took a quick breath and was stunned by the cold as it hit his sinuses. He felt as if all the mucus in his muzzle had frozen instantly. His teeth rattled against the plastic flashlight. The cold burned his eyes; tears leaked onto his cheeks and froze.

Kanti climbed a little higher and found another hatch. This hatch had the sensor on the other side as well. He wondered if he'd be able to string a wire across the leads even if the sensor had been accessible. He hated the thought of removing the mitts.

His body started to shake with a violent palsy, and he feared it'd knock him from the holds. Panic rose in him, but he pushed it back down and climbed a little higher.

The next hatch was short and wide. He'd have thought it odd, if he weren't in such a rush to get out of the cold. This hatch had a sensor on the baffle side. His paws shook out of control, but on closer inspection, he could see that the sensor was corroded and cracked. One of the rusted wires had broken free long ago and was no longer even connected. No one would notice any change when he opened this hatch.

He grabbed the hand-wheel and pulled as hard as he could. It didn't move at first, but then turned suddenly. Kanti spilled through the open hatch and slammed it shut behind him with a kick of his boot. Without even cranking it shut, he fell to the floor and curled up in a ball.

The mitts discarded, he cupped his paws over his nose and genitals, trying to warm them up. He shook uncontrollably for ten whole minutes before he could even lock the hatch behind him.

Never again. Never again, Kanti swore ... *without protective clothing, at least.*

Chapter 6: Skeleton Crew

Kanti found himself in a tiny airlock. The indicators on the other door all shone blue. He had no idea what lay beyond the portal, but at least it wasn't vacuum. He punched the button and cycled the lock.

Kanti groaned as the sulfur hit his nose. The stench was horrible – worse even than the recycler bay – but at least the strange chamber he found himself in was warm, hot even. He found himself panting. The room was short, perhaps only a meter and a half high, but it extended far into the distance in all directions.

The gravity was extreme here. He struggled to cross the room on his belly, but there was no way he was going to turn around and go back into the bulkhead.

In the flashlight beam he saw six different gravity generators, arranged in a circle. He shrugged at the strange sight and crawled on. As he moved, he found the gravity pulling him in different directions. The strange sensation of being pulled this way and that was extremely disorienting and made him feel a little nauseated.

After crawling for what felt like an hour, he found the far side of the enormous chamber. He hated being unable to smell anything other than sulfur. His fur was filthy, and he was exhausted, but this wasn't a good place to rest. No hatches exited the room, but a row of rungs led up into another tube.

Climbing the rungs in a high gravity environment was a lot tougher than he had anticipated. His arms were leaden. The tube went on and on, and he found no place to get off and rest. Instead, he locked his knees and leaned against the back wall of the tube periodically to give his biceps a chance to recover. His forearms were burning up, and the hot, sulfurous air was draining his strength. He hadn't really climbed all that high, but if he fell, the extra gravity would make crashing to the deck below as devastating as if he had toppled from a far greater height.

Kanti climbed a bit more and finally found an access panel. But unlike the others, this was just a simple plastic cover concealing the tube from the room beyond. He knew it'd pop right out if he pressed against it; no latches secured it.

"Enough!" a voice shouted in Krakun. The plastic cover rattled with the sound. All the cubs aboard the White Flower II were taught to read and speak Krakun, despite having almost no opportunities for most of the crew to use it.

Out of curiosity, Kanti had downloaded a couple of undubbed movies from Krakuntec. The special effects were incredible, but the movies themselves were nearly unwatchable. The stories weren't intended for geroo audiences, and the plots were just too "alien" to make any sense of at all. He had almost wished that he couldn't understand the words.

The shouting startled Kanti, and he missed the next handhold. He scrambled wildly for a moment as he visualized falling back against - and then through - the plastic panel, and found himself clinging to a bundle of cables running up the length of the tube. His heart pounded wildly, and he breathed so hard that he feared he'd hyperventilate.

Someone was talking in the next compartment. No, arguing? Ever so gently, he pressed his ear against the plastic panel, being very careful not to dislodge it. The conversation outside the tube continued for quite a while. He knew it was wrong to eavesdrop, but he just couldn't help himself.

Kanti could make out almost nothing, but a couple of sentences did stand out from the rest.

"I don't care if you have to save semen samples of all your males and reduce down to a skeleton crew of breeding-age females," the huge voice boomed. "I ... will ... not ... lose ... this ... ship."

———————— § ————————

Kanti hurried back to his apartment as soon as he found an airlock leading out. He showered away the filth. He tried to wash away the memories.

He had heard of a skeleton crew before, of course. The ghost story was shared by circles of male cubs ever since the very beginning of the voyage. The tale told of a generation ship that could no longer produce oxygen. The crew's males recycled themselves in order to save their wives and daughters, and the vessel limped along on only the oxygen produced by the crops. When male cubs were born, the crew allowed them to live only until they reached puberty, when they could help resupply the ship's dwindling stocks of semen.

The story was a very frightening when told properly – especially for a male cub nearing puberty!

He lay awake in his bed, shivering slightly.

That had to have been the commissioner arguing. He had only ever seen Sarsuk once, but no other krakun ever came aboard.

So why the talk of a skeleton crew?

Kanti realized he was panicking, and the apartment's dark and awful closeness weren't helping. The familiar smells were not reassuring. Instead they made him feel trapped – buried alive.

Was the ship broken? Were they all going to die? If something was wrong with the recycler, he'd know, wouldn't he? Surely the captain would assign every available technician to help out. He would have seen them there, messing with it while he worked.

He'd heard talk of the trinity going down for maintenance, but he presumed it'd be no different than any maintenance cycles in the past. Now he feared the worst.

Kanti fumbled in his pack and found the air monitor by touch. He turned it on, and the blue indicator lit. He turned it back off.

He put it back in the bag, only to take it out again. Blue. He turned it off once more.

Would it be painful, he wondered, *to suffocate in your sleep?*

He couldn't sleep. He worried that he'd never sleep again.

Kanti pulled out his strand and searched for "skeleton crew." The screen displayed a list of many documents and a couple of videos. His mind raced frantically, and he was far too anxious to read. He tapped on a link to a video.

The video was the tale of doomed freighter that had marooned its captain on a planetoid. The remainder of the crew had perished in the crash. Years later, the skeleton crew of a forsaken generation ship rescued him, starving and half-mad with loneliness.

Like most low-budget geroo videos, the acting was amateur, the story weak, and the sets unconvincing.

Kanti blinked in silence while he watched.

Apparently this tale was also a porno.

"Oh well," he sighed. "I've already paid for the download."

Chapter 7: A Table for Two

The morning came, and the air monitor continued to blink blue whenever Kanti turned it on. He went to work, and soon the drudgery of operating a dozer replaced the fading terror and worry from the night before.

"Here you go, Saina," Tish said, tapping her strand against Kanti's.

"Thanks," he mumbled, staring at the number. It wasn't enough. Well, it would cover rent, but that was about it. Once that was paid, he'd be reduced to eating in the mess hall every night until his next paycheck. He didn't have enough for groceries.

Kanti desperately needed a raise. He put a paw over his eyes. Actually, he needed *Saina* to get a raise, since his boss thought Kanti was Saina. Saina was never going to get a raise.

What a mess.

Truthfully, he reminded himself, the problem wasn't Saina. His problem was really the apartment. Despite the apartment's location on an undesirable deck, it was large enough for a couple of small families to share. And here he was, keeping it all to himself.

He needed to give it up, but if he did, could he ever get another? Was he brave enough to sign a lease? No, it would be far safer to share the apartment with a family - or two. If he could just share the rent, then he'd have lots of credits left over each month.

But how?

The apartment was just too full. Unless he could get his mom's junk hauled away, there was no way he could get a roommate.

Weekly trash pick-up would only take a maximum of two bags per address, and he needed to get rid of ... . Kanti's brain froze up trying to imagine just how many bags it would take to empty the place. A thousand? Ten thousand? He had no idea.

Why did you do this to me, Mom? The question was pointless. He knew the answer. His mother had always been a "collector" – she got irate if you ever said "hoarder" in her presence – but when her mate died, the collecting got way out of control. Every day, Kanti came home from work to find more and more junk piled up on top of the old junk.

Kanti needed to rent a truck. Then he could drive loads of trash down to the recycler himself.

He stared at the number on the screen again.

He couldn't afford a truck.

Kanti was not amused by the irony of being a "garbage man" whose life was drowning in garbage.

"You are the only guy I know," Saina chuckled, "who can look tragic on pay-day." He put his arm around Kanti's shoulders.

"It's not enough," Kanti mumbled, still staring at the strand.

"No, it never is!" Saina laughed. "Let me buy you a drink."

Kanti shook his head and started walking out of Recycler Bay Two. "Thanks, but no. I'm headed to the mess hall to grab some chow. 'Going out' isn't in the budget this week."

With his arm around his friend's shoulders, Saina turned Kanti away from the door. Apart from the vast difference in shape, the pair could be brothers. They were the same height, had the same eyes and similar ears. Saina had the smooth coat and Kanti had the scruffy one.

Saina led Kanti out of the blue zone and onto the orange deck.

Kanti looked nervously around and let out an unconscious chitter. Supervisors permitted the workers to step paw into the orange zone, but only if they followed procedure. Everyone knew that you had to log it into Taskmaster and get an "all clear" before you could leave your dozer.

The computer kept careful track of all the dozers on deck. If an operator ignored Taskmaster's warnings and drove too close to an area containing a pedestrian, the system automatically shut down the vehicle's ignition as a precaution. Although it would be hard to miss the sound of an approaching dozer, that wasn't enough to ensure a pedestrian's safety in the orange zone. He needed the computer to know he was there. Workers couldn't count on being spotted by an operator before being reduced from "crew member" to the less-desirable classification of "organics."

"Stop being such a mewling cub," Saina grunted. "I gotta' show you something."

He led Kanti out to the distant corner of the deck, where workers stacked aluminum scrap into evenly spaced heaps that towered five meters tall at their peak. "I chose a spot as far away from the organics as possible, so the smell wouldn't be so bad," he explained.

Hidden behind the very last heap was a cozy, little grotto containing two soiled but comfortable-looking chairs, a huge spool of tubing that substituted for a table, and a contraption made of pots and tubes.

Kanti stared for many long moments with jaw agape.

"Well?" Saina nudged him with an elbow. "What do you think?"

"I think you've lost your mind," the shaggy geroo replied. "What's going to happen when someone rolls through here with a dozer to gather all the aluminum?"

Saina shrugged. "Everything in life is fleeting. But for now, you and I have our own little, private club." With the twist of a valve, the chubby, young geroo filled a cracked mug from the still. "Cocktail?" he asked with a grin.

Kanti looked around once more, but the sector was empty. He reluctantly accepted the cup with a smile, set his strand on the table, and tried to relax into one of the chairs.

The geroo were never without their strands. They were more than just a means of communication; the devices acted as their money, their keys, their records, and their access to the network. Since the White Flower II's departure, strands came to symbolize the "connectedness" of all the geroo aboard. The strands wove the crew – and even the crews of the other ships – together into a gigantic, patch-work quilt.

It wasn't surprising, perhaps, that removing your communicator in private company became more than just a custom. It was expected etiquette – a way of saying, "you have my attention."

Saina poured himself a mug.

"I looked for you when I finished dancing with Jasmi," Saina said, "but you and her friend had vanished." He grinned and winked. "What was her name? The white-furred gal with the cute brown spot?" He motioned with a finger around one of his eyes.

Kanti shrugged. "No idea."

Saina yarped a loud laugh. "You rogue! I had no idea. ..."

"She bailed the moment I tried talking to her," Kanti said, deflating Saina's grin. "I went home alone."

Saina sighed and tapped his mug against Kanti's. They both drank.

Kanti shuddered involuntarily and tried to blink back the tears. He felt as if his throat were on fire.

"Smooth, huh?" Saina said, smacking his lips. "The fruit I used was ... well, way past its prime, but distillation should kill any germs. ..."

Kanti stared at him, trying to form words. He wondered how many brain cells this swill had just killed. "Have you tried using it as a degreaser?" he gasped at long last.

Saina grinned and refilled the mugs.

Kanti thanked him and stared a long time at the clear liquid in his mug without braving another taste. "How long have we been friends?"

Saina shrugged. "Dunno'. Three years? Four?"

Kanti sighed, and Saina stared at him. "I've been keeping a secret from you," the scruffy geroo admitted. "Well, from the whole ship, really."

Saina got up to fiddle with the still.

"And I feel really bad about it. You're my best friend ... my only friend." He turned to stare at Saina, but the chubby geroo didn't appear to be paying attention. He sighed.

Saina's strand began to chime, and Kanti grumbled to himself about the interruption. He glanced over at the display. "Someone named 'Chendra'?"

Saina shook his head and continued to adjust the tubing.

The chimes continued.

"Aren't you gonna' answer that?"

"Hells, no." Saina shook his head again. "You can talk to her if you want. 15113."

Kanti stared at the device as it blinked and chimed. For some weird reason, it irritated him. No one ever called *him*. Saina was the only one to ever send him a message, and that was usually just where to meet him for drinks. He grabbed the device and punched in Saina's access code, ready to bark at the caller that Saina was too busy to talk.

The name was replaced with an image of the most beautiful geroo that Kanti had ever seen. She had smooth, brown fur; large, brown eyes; small ears; and high cheekbones. Kanti instantly forgot how to form words.

The girl looked as shocked as Kanti did. "Oh, my goodness! You picked up! I was just going to leave you another message."

Kanti just stared. He smiled a little at her. Her eyes sparkled at him.

"You look great! I mean, really, really great!"

"I ... I do?" he gasped.

She beamed happily at him and nodded, then noticed the heap of aluminum behind him. "Are you at work? I didn't mean to bother you. I was just going to leave a message and see if you'd come over for dinner on the fifth."

A text prompt appeared on the screen that read, "Dinner @ Chendra's on the 5th. Confirm?"

Saina's head popped up, and he waved his arms emphatically. *No!* he mouthed, but Kanti wasn't paying him any attention.

"I'd love to!" Kanti said, happily making a little circle gesture around the text prompt, adding the event to the calendar.

"Really?! Oh my goodness!" Chendra nearly shouted.

"Are you kidding? I wouldn't miss it for the whole ship." He smiled the largest smile that he could ever recall.

Saina slapped his forehead with both paws.

"Okay, I won't keep you. I'll see you on the fifth!"

"Great, it's a date!"

The screen went dark with a message about the call being terminated, and Kanti continued to stare at the screen in a daze.

"What the hells was that for?" Saina shouted after a long pause.

"Huh, what?" Kanti mumbled. His mouth moved, but his brain had not yet engaged.

"I don't know why you're pissed at me, but setting me up to visit Chendra isn't funny!" He broke a piece off the still and stared at it in his paw. "Arrgh!" he shouted.

Kanti stared at Saina's strand. The new appointment flashed to remind Saina of the event he scheduled.

"What the hells is wrong with me?" Kanti mumbled, burying his face in his paws.

The pair hung out in silence for a while, waiting for Saina's degreaser to lighten the mood.

Saina finally spoke up. "You don't need to tell me your 'secret.' I already know."

Kanti's ears shot up. "You ... you do?"

Saina nodded. "I think everyone's suspected it. You never go out on dates. You never even look at females."

"What? Um, wait, what?" Kanti struggled. "Yes, I do!"

"It's okay, buddy, I won't judge you. We can find a guy you like, instead."

"No! I'm not gay!" Kanti shouted. "I'm illegal!" He slapped a paw over his mouth and looked around, terrified that someone else might have heard him.

Saina seemed unfocused and confused. "Um, what?" He scratched at his chin. "Like a fugitive?"

"No," Kanti whispered. "I was never supposed to be born."

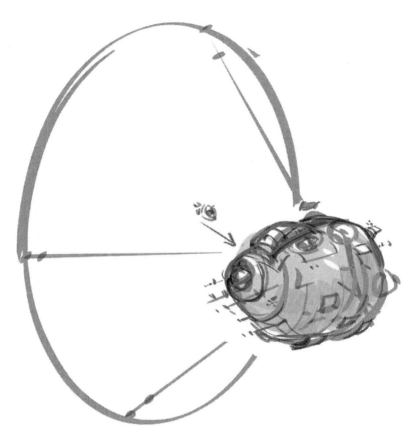

Sarsuk's shuttle emerges from the gate, to dock with the White Flower II.

The White Flower II

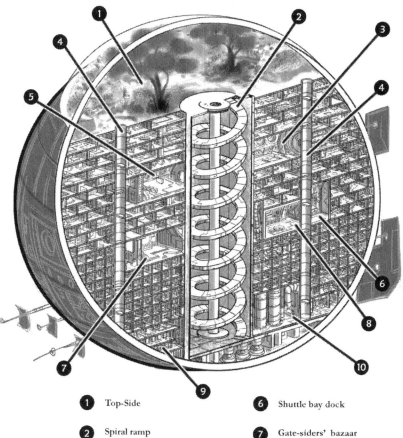

1	Top-Side	**6**	Shuttle bay dock
2	Spiral ramp	**7**	Gate-siders' bazaar
3	Engineering	**8**	Sarsuk' s quarters
4	Gravity wells	**9**	Barracks
5	Bridge	**10**	Recycler bay 2

Chapter 8: The Trinity

Kanti stared out of the grungy viewing port, waiting. Most of the crew didn't get excited to see the gate powered up or down, not after seeing it once or twice, at least. But this never got old for Kanti.

Besides, the shutdown was in the forefront of his mind – this time. He wondered if he should have told Saina what he'd overheard. If he should repeat what the commissioner had said. *No.* It was bad enough admitting that he was illegal to his best friend. He didn't need to reveal his strange obsession as well.

What if Saina wanted to come along on one of his outings? Kanti didn't want to share that with anyone.

He tried to push the worry from his mind and thought back to a happier past. His mother took him down here as a cub to watch the gate powered up. He sat on her shoulders and stared for minutes, afraid to blink – afraid he'd miss it. How he missed those simple days!

His strand beeped with a ship-wide announcement. He glanced at the screen.

From: Engineering
To: All crew of the White Flower II
Subject: Trinity Maintenance

As mentioned previously, engineering will take trinity offline for scheduled maintenance, starting shortly after Commissioner Sarsuk departs from his regular visit — probably around *1400 hours, today*.

Maintenance should take approximately one hour.

Engineering will power the trinity back up as soon as possible, but for safety reasons, it must remain offline for a minimum of 17 hours to discharge fully. We anticipate restoration of service, at roughly *0700 hours*. The crew will be advised.

As with every outage, the crew will abide by *standard outage protocol* to minimize the consumption of electricity, fuel, water, and oxygen:
- No cooking
- No combustion of any sort (including smoking)
- No use of heavy machinery unless deemed mission-critical
- As always, any unused equipment should be powered off

The message continued, but Kanti didn't bother scrolling down. The same message posted each time there was an outage, and he had read it before. He glanced at the time. It was nearly 1400 hours now.

Back out the spaceport, Kanti stared at the blinking, yellow lights demarcating the edge of the gate. The gate itself, a loop of aluminum over seven kilometers wide, was otherwise invisible in the inky black depths of space. The black space and specks of starlight within the circle of the gate looked no different than the black space and specks of starlight beyond its edge, but it *was* different. The green and orange planet at the center of the loop was Krakuntec - a planet nearly 1,000 light years away from the White Flower II.

Kanti watched as the commissioner's shuttle slid silently towards Krakuntec. The ship crossed through the gate and was transported instantly to that distant part of the galaxy without crossing through the intervening space. On the bridge, up on deck nine, the communications officer on duty confirmed a safe transit and cleared engineering to begin their maintenance.

Of the three legs of the trinity – the gate, the drive, and the recycler – the gate left Kanti truly awestruck. How could even krakun technology connect their gate with its sister-gate in orbit around Krakuntec? It made his head hurt when he thought about it too hard.

The lights surrounding the gate blinked red, and in an instant, Krakuntec vanished. The stars shimmered and jumped to new locations. Kanti knew that the gate was off now, and the loop of metal tubing that formed the gate was now merely a loop of metal. Flying through the gate now wouldn't take you to the Krakuntec star system, it would just take you through the loop.

Simultaneously, the drive and the recycler powered down.

The drive had a lot in common with the gate. The drive had the power to transport the ship itself through space, and like the gate it did so without having to pass through the intervening space. But instead of transporting the ship one thousand light years, each jump moved the ship by a fraction of a meter. It could, however, perform the jump a billion times a second.

By making tiny jumps over and over again, the drive moved the vessel at a little under the speed of light. But since the ship didn't accelerate or decelerate, the ship's occupants felt no relativistic effects. Time passage aboard the ship was no different than that on Krakuntec. The stars ahead didn't shift blue and the ones behind didn't shift red. This peculiar leg of the trinity tricked relativity by keeping the ship motionless for a billionth of a second and then moving it instantaneously.

Objectively, the drive was even more impressive than the gate. But even near the speed of light, it took several years to drive the generation ship from one star system to the next. It was hard to get excited – as a passenger, at least – about journey legs measured in years.

Although the trinity served three different functions, it was a single entity. The crew had no way to shut off any one leg of it and keep the others online. Was that a quirk of physics or prescribed by krakun design? Geroo had hotly debated that ever since the beginning of the journey. But one thing was certain: there was no practical way for a crew to steal a generation ship.

If the White Flower II ever defied Planetary Acquisitions, the company merely had to deactivate its sister gate in orbit around Krakuntec. Without both gates operational, the White Flower II's gate did not function. And without the gate, there could be no drive or recycler.

Life without the recycler might be possible, but without the drive, the ship would be left adrift. It wouldn't be much of an existence, waiting in deep space to see if the company would send a destroyer to reclaim its property – probably leaving the crew behind in the vacuum.

"Thought I'd find you here," Saina said. "Come on, the party's just starting."

"I told you, I'm broke." Kanti shook his head.

"The 'grotto' it is!" Saina put his arm around the scruffy geroo's shoulders and led him back toward Recycler Bay Two.

Without the trinity, the White Flower II was little more than a gigantic aluminum can drifting across the fabric of space. Most of the crew was either unable to work, or prohibited from working to conserve resources. Of those that could still function, most used the shutdown as an excuse not to work. And since it was impossible for the commissioner to visit while the gate was offline, shutdowns were some of the greatest ship-wide holidays that the crew had.

"So what's it like being a non-person?" Saina asked.

"I'm not ..." Kanti looked nervously around and lowered his voice to a whisper. "I'm not a non-person."

Saina shrugged. "Well, you are to the company."

Kanti looked dejected and wondered whether it had been wise to share his secret with his friend. "It's ... it's like walking on eggs all the time. Every payday I'm worried that some computer somewhere will realize that I'm not on the crew roster. That some programmer will add instructions to cross-check it. Every time I buy something, I worry. If I do well at work, I worry about being considered for a promotion. I worry if I mess up too."

Kanti covered his eyes with his paw. He had never really tried to analyze how he felt. His world had always been this way, at least since his parents told him as a cub. "I'd love to change apartments, but the one I have is leased in my parents' names. I guess no one cares who pays the rent, but what if I try to lease one myself? Will they look into my past to see if I'm reliable and not find any history at all? Will someone stumble on my secret?"

"Well, maybe if you discussed it with an administrator, they could get you a birth token?"

"No way!" Kanti pulled away from Saina and lowered his voice back to a whisper. "I've searched around in the records. There's no news stories of anyone ever trying to get legal after they were born. I'm not going to be the first. What if they said that I didn't deserve any of the years I've had so far? I can't even prove how many years I've had.

"What if everyone found out? Would they think that I have no soul since I didn't inherit a token when someone was recycled?"

Saina put his arm back around Kanti's shoulders. "Well, look at the lit side ... at least you won't have to worry about getting an orange pill for your sixtieth birthday." He gave him a lopsided smile.

Kanti tried to pull away, but Saina refused to let go. It was difficult to be glum as they walked along to the recycler bay. Everyone everywhere was having a good time; eating, drinking, laughing, dancing, and playing music. Kanti managed a feeble smile of his own. "Well, if I make it that long ... somehow ... I'll come to your sixtieth and wish you good journey."

Saina yarped a laugh. "Not me. I only get fifty-five."

Kanti stared at the chubby geroo. "You lost five years? How horrible!"

Saina shrugged. "The last five are the worst five. They're the 'getting up five times a night to urinate' years. They're the 'throwing your back out by sneezing' years. They're the 'remembering how nice your mate *used to* smell' years!" He yarped another loud laugh.

Kanti looked around, but no one paid them any attention. "How did you lose them?"

Saina laughed and punched his access code into the device on his shoulder. "It's a long, sad story," he said as the four gigantic quadrants of the door to the recycler bay ground slowly open. "I'm going to need a drink while I tell it."

"How am I supposed to brood about all our miserable lives when you keep making me so damn happy?"

#013

Setting: Hayven Celestia (10 Thousand Miles Up)
Characters: Ateri, Jakari

Chapter 9: Collateral Damage

The room was a mess, with bedding and possessions lumped on the floor – the signs of a perpetually busy pair. But worse than the clutter was the smell. Although not yet offensive, the apartment had gained an aroma of neglect and sex. The walls were bare. If any food remained in the cabinets or refrigerator, it would no longer be edible.

Jakari smiled in post-coital bliss. Her left cheek rested against Ateri's strong, furry chest. She listened to his slow breaths and the furious pounding of his heart. With a claw, she traced circles across her mate's belly. They were quite the pair. He with his jet black pelt, strong and somber. She with her white pelt, fluffy, curvy, and loquacious.

Their duties kept them working non-stop. The apartment had become a refuge for sleep and bonding only. "The marketplace is getting as crazy as a dockworker," she said. "It's going to be a great party. Let's get out and have some fun."

Ateri opened his eye and lifted his head slightly off the pillow. "I thought we were having fun here."

"We *were*, and now I'd like to go out and have some fun that involves music and dancing."

The captain smiled and dropped his head back against the pillow.

"What's wrong, hon?" she asked. Jakari turned to rest an arm across his torso and her chin against the back of her wrist. "You've been moody ever since your conference with Commissioner Sarsuk."

Ateri sighed deeply. She could always tell when he tried to keep something from her. "The commissioner doubts the accuracy of our census."

Jakari rolled her eyes. "Of course he does. He doubts everything that shows you are doing a great job.

"The census, of all things!" She snorted a laugh. "If he'd like, we can all file past him and he can count us himself. One geroo ... two geroo ... three ..." she mocked. "That would make for a very thrilling cycle, I'm sure."

"No, Sarsuk thinks that there are geroo aboard who aren't on the ship's roster." Ateri sighed. "He thinks they're dodging the census, and he wants suggestions on how to count everyone, even those who don't want to be counted."

"That big, infuriating toad!" Jakari dropped her face against Ateri's chest. "He's been commissioner over geroo for four hundred years and he still thinks of us as kerrati! Is he expecting to pull open a panel and find geroo hiding in there, nibbling on wiring?" She showed Ateri her teeth and made a chittering sound to imitate the rat-like creatures that had infested the granaries on Gerootec.

Ateri yarped a loud laugh and put his paw over her face to make her stop. "No, I think he fears that some of us might be hiding in plain sight; acting as crew members, doing our jobs, but not actually included on the crew roster."

"Could we get a head-count by having the network count strands? Everyone has one, and they're all unique."

The captain shook his head. "I thought about that, but some of us have multiple communicators, and it wouldn't count cubs and geroo in utero."

"Well, I guess you could have everyone fill out a census of their families, friends, co-workers, students, and school-mates. That would probably get everyone counted a half-dozen different ways." Jakari said with a smile. "The software guys could crunch the results to remove as many duplicates as possible. Then the census crew would just have to follow up on questionable duplicates or missing entries instead of the usual head-counting."

Ateri nodded, "Yeah, I think that would work. The crew might resist it and feel that the company is digging into their personal lives. ..."

"Well, it is, isn't it? You'd have to treat it as any other assignment. Either punish them for non-compliance or reward them for cooperation."

"Reward them?" Ateri nodded, deep in thought. "That might work. We could make it a game."

"Problem solved." Jakari got out of bed and started getting dressed. She clipped on her necklace and prompted her mate to help her with the bracelet she enjoyed wearing on her tail. "So we can go dancing now?"

The captain swung his legs over the side of the bed. He rested his elbows on his knees and his face in his paws. "We need to work on some contingency plans. These need to be kept quiet. No one –"

Jakari rolled her eyes. "In all the years we have known each other –"

"These more so than others," Ateri cut her off without looking up. "If the commissioner determines that our census has been low in the past, he may demand that we recycle crew-members who still have years remaining."

The bracelet clattered to the floor, forgotten. "Would that really be necessary? Couldn't we just delay issuing some birth tokens to Happy Couples?"

Ateri said nothing.

There was a pregnant pause before she put her soft paws on his shoulders. "The crew trusts you ... I trust you ... but such an order ..." She shook her head. "It'd be a lot to ask of them."

Ateri nodded somberly. "It would. If Sarsuk demands it, I will debate it. I will offer every alternative we can prepare. I will fight him with every erg of energy I can muster, but I doubt it will matter. We must be prepared to carry out such an order, somehow."

Jakari sat down beside her mate and stared ahead, her expression as bare as the wall itself. She habitually kept herself to her mate's right side; she slept on the right, she walked on his right. She had done it so long that she did it without conscious effort. She sat to his left, now. She didn't want him looking at her.

"I don't know how many geroo might be involved. We need plans for any number." He cleared his throat. "If we must recycle fifty geroo, then perhaps we could choose the oldest, those who have the fewest cycles left anyhow. That might cause the least harm to morale. We will need a list of crew-members sorted by cycles remaining."

Jakari silently mouthed the word *fifty*.

"If he demands that we recycle five hundred, then we will need to be more creative. We will need to know who is crucial in each department, and who is ..." Ateri stopped himself, but she knew the word that hung on his lips. He had almost said **expendable**. "The crew members whose loss would impact us the least.

"Do we sacrifice everyone who turned out to be illegitimate? Mobs might demand it. But what if many of them work in the same department and recycling them all will leave us short-staffed? Do we dare grant any of them citizenship at the cost of someone else who was supposed to be here? Since we don't know who is illegitimate, we need flexible plans, and not hard lists. Do we cull convicts first and give priority to everyone with a clean record? Who will we leave orphaned? What's the minimum age we'd consider for recycling?"

Despite her uncanny ability to mask her feelings in public, when alone with her mate, Jakari left those defenses untapped. Large tears began to soak the white fur on her cheeks. She tried to push the images out of her mind, but they wouldn't be banished. In her mind's eye, mothers threw their cubs into the recycler. Bulldozers pushed struggling crowds into the deep violet glow.

"If he demands that we recycle five thousand ..."

"That's half the crew!" she shouted.

He paused a long time. She couldn't be angry with him. She knew that he cared as deeply for the crew as she did. He was just better at suppressing his feelings. She knew that deep down, behind all of the walls had he built up, he felt the same hot, angry, frustrated emotions. He felt helpless, too.

"At that point, we will need to worry about maintaining our genetic diversity. We need to chart a path to bounce back and return to a viable population."

"Seventy-five hundred geroo ..." He shook his head, at a loss. "I guess we need to figure out just how deep he could cut us. How many crew members must we have to carry on ... to ever hope that we could return to a full complement some day."

Ateri's strand beeped from somewhere underneath the bed. He dropped to his paws and knees, swinging his head in broad arcs, searching the floor with his remaining eye for where it could have fallen.

"Bata'ho!" he answered it at last. "I'm glad you got my message, and I'm sorry to interrupt your holiday." Ateri began to pace furiously around the cluttered apartment as he spoke into the small device. "What do we know of the bio-limit that the krakun set for this ship? – Yes, I know the number, but how did they come up with it? Is there a safety factor, or is six hundred thousand a hard limit? – Do cubs count less than adults? What about pregnant females? – Is there a way to gauge what our bio-load on the ship is at any given moment in time? – Yes, I know about the death-spiral, but can we tell how close we are to the tipping-point?"

Ateri nodded for a while, listening intently. Eventually, he looked over at his mate, still sitting on the side of the bed. He tapped the mute button. "We've made contingency plans before. Many times. Ninety-nine point nine percent of all contingency plans are never needed, and these are likely no different. We need to do our jobs. We need to do our duty."

Jakari closed her eyes and nodded. He was right.

"Think not just of who'd need to go, but how we can communicate this with the crew. If there was ever a mutiny, well ..."

She imagined the alternatives, and completed his thought. "Sarsuk might give up on us all and split the crew from another ship to take over the White Flower II. I'm sure they'd jump at the chance to get ten *thousand* additional birth tokens."

Ateri nodded and turned back to the screen. That summed it up. "Are you still there? – No, I don't think it's just a matter of chemistry. Think bigger. Are we using up food faster than we can grow it? – Are we exceeding the capacity of the recycler? Is the air quality starting to decay? What about water? Electricity? – What about social factors? How many geroo can work together in this environment before we lose control of the crew?"

Without another word, Jakari sat down at a dusty terminal and began to sift through the crew roster.

Chapter 10: Pariah

"I didn't know that you still live with your folks," Saina said, filling two mugs with degreaser from the still. He smiled and shook his head, surprised at his best friend. "You never mentioned them."

Kanti shrugged. "I don't; not anymore. My dad fell off of a scaffolding five years ago. Broke his back."

Saina winced. "Ouch. Can't krakun medical technology fix a severed spine?"

"They can." Kanti sighed. "But the doctor said it'd take years of rehab before he'd walk again. I guess the company administrator decided that he couldn't take that long off of work. Instead, they gave him three days to get his affairs in order."

Saina lowered his eyes without anything to add. He growled in frustration. The recycler bay fell silent. The lights were dim.

"My mom, just ..." Kanti searched for words. "I guess she just drifted away after my dad got recycled. She ... died about the time you started working here."

"I'm so sorry," Saina said quietly. He felt awkward for bringing it up. "I didn't mean to pry."

"No, it's okay. I've never really talked to anyone about them. I just keep it ... bottled up, worried that someone might ask questions that lead them back to me."

"Do you think that there's anyone else on board who was born without a token?"

Kanti shrugged. "No idea. It's not as if we have a club. But if the captain ever found out about someone like me, then he dealt with it quietly. I've done plenty of searches and never found a whisper of it in any of the logs."

Silence stretched.

"So how did you lose five years? What the hells did you do?"

Saina laughed and flopped down in the dirty, tattered chair. He sipped at his drink and licked his lips. "You might not realize it, but I used to be quite the party animal. I'd go to a new one every week. I'd dance and drink until my next shift started."

Kanti gave him a sideways look.

"Well, you could at least pretend to be shocked," Saina said with a grin.

"You invited me to one. It was your first day at the recycler."

Saina snapped his pads and nodded enthusiastically. "Right! I forgot all about that. My last party."

"I didn't go," Kanti said, hanging his head.

"No one did." Saina grinned some more. "Don't feel bad."

"I should have gone. It was very nice of you to invite me. No one ever does, but you said that your address was seven-nineteen."

The chubby geroo stared at his friend. "You still remember my address? That was years ago!"

Kanti shrugged. "I've always had a great memory. I never write anything down. My folks thought I'd become captain or an engineer or something, but I was useless in school. Anyhow, I knew you had to be screwing with me. No one works at the recycler if they can afford to live up on seven."

Now it was Saina's turn to hang his head. "I used to be an economist – working up on five."

Kanti blinked in shock. He stared at his friend as if they had never met previously. "An economist?"

"Yeah, I worked up costs of living and balanced wages for company jobs." Kanti's expression was still blank, so Saina continued to explain. "So, if we had too many farmers and not enough geroo driving dozers, I'd reduce how much farmers earn and increase how much money you'd make for working at the recycler. Eventually, more of us would go to work driving dozers and fewer would choose to grow crops."

"So, you could get me a raise?" Kanti asked hopefully.

Saina yarped a laugh and slapped his paw down on the chair's arm. "Not anymore, I couldn't." He took a big drink and stared up at the ceiling, reminiscing. "My downfall was at a party ... one that was even wilder than all the rest. It was thrown by a friend of a friend ... a guy who lives up on *three*. I'd never seen such a beautiful apartment ... and the females ..." he sighed and fell back in his seat, his ears way out to the sides. "Each one smelled better than the last.

"The booze flowed like a river, and I dove right in. And I'm not talking about rot-gut like this swill – it was as if you were drinking cool candy that warmed you slowly from the inside." Saina winked. "I don't remember much of that night, but I know that I had the time of my life.

"I spoke my mind that night. I let it all out. I had no inhibitions whatsoever." Saina stared at the bottom of his empty mug for a moment before refilling it. "Two security officers woke me up the next morning and dragged me before the judge." He yarped a laugh. "I was still so drunk that they had to hold me upright during sentencing."

"Sentencing?" Kanti gasped.

Saina scratched at the short, creme-colored fur on his double chin. "Like I said, five years."

Kanti's mouth hung open. "They took away five years for something you said at a party?"

"It was a great party." Saina put his ears to the side in a grin. Sadness passed behind his eyes, and he shrugged it off.

Kanti's ears drooped in a frown, but he said nothing.

"When I finally sobered up, I tried to hire a lawyer to appeal my case, but no one would even talk to me. I went to work and found my personal items in a box."

Kanti shook his head in disbelief.

"But the 'best' part ..." Saina explained, "the 'best' part was when I opened up the job listings on my strand, and driving a dozer was the only position the network said I was qualified for.

"I don't know who overheard me talking at that party, but whoever he was, he was a geroo of real power. He wanted me to learn my place - to humble me. I was so shocked that it took months of working here before it finally sank in, before I finally believed that it had happened to me."

Saina sighed. "I've been a pariah ever since. That party you missed was going to be my farewell to the high decks. A couple of friends stopped in for a moment to say goodbye before they too stopped returning my calls."

The pair was silent for the longest time before Kanti broke the spell. "What did you say, to deserve all that?"

Saina grinned again. "I complained about our slavery to the krakun."

Artwork ©2014 Rick Griffin

Chapter 11: Overpopulation

"Does anyone know what day tomorrow is?" Yargo asked her class. A few cubs looked up, but most continued to draw quietly. "Tomorrow is a very special holiday. It's called 'Visitor Day.' Can anyone tell me why we call it that?"

Yargo waited for an answer, but none of the cubs raised a paw. "Visitor Day celebrates the day when the krakun first visited our planet, Gerootec. Back then, the geroo celebrated a lot of different holidays. They had a holiday when it was time to plant their crops, a harvest holiday, a holiday when winter began, and one for the beginning of summer. ... But we don't celebrate any of those holidays anymore. Does anyone know why?"

Yargo looked around the room, and a pair of bright, green eyes met her own. "Do you know why, Kanti?"

The scruffy-furred cub looked down immediately, but the whole class had already turned to face him. "Um ... um ..." he mumbled. "Because we live on a spaceship?"

"That's right!" his teacher answered.

Kanti's smile spread across his ears. The normally quiet cub looked so proud.

"Now that we live on the White Flower II, there are no seasons," Yargo explained. "It doesn't get hot or cold. We plant our crops every day, and we harvest them every day, too. That way, we always have enough food for everyone.

"Does anyone know what sort of things the krakun gave us when they visited Gerootec?"

Yargo looked around, but the class was pretty still. Colorful chalk drawings of families, planets, and even a couple of krakun decorated the walls. The cubs were paying attention, but she didn't see anyone wanting to answer. "The krakun gave us medicine and doctors. Did you know that, class? Before the first Visitor Day, when geroo got sick or hurt, everyone would just hope that they got well. But now we have doctors that we can go to when we get sick, and they make us all better.

"Does anyone else know something that the krakun gave us on Visitor Day?"

A girl with yellow eyes and a golden pelt stood, uncertain and looking down.

"Yes, Rina? Can you name something?"

Rina looked up for a moment before spurting "Spaceships?"

"Very good answer, Rina!" Yargo gave the girl her friendliest smile. "The krakun actually gave us spaceships the second time they visited us. That's the other holiday we celebrate. Do you know what we call that holiday?"

Rina shook her head for a moment before she nodded. "X Day?"

"Very close, Rina!" Yargo clapped her paws together. "It's called Exodus. The day our ancestors left Gerootec.

"Can anyone else name something that the visitors gave us on Visitor Day?" She gave the cubs a little longer to answer. "No? Well, the krakun gave us school. Before the krakun visited Gerootec, cubs helped their parents on their farms. It was very hard work! But now you get to go to school instead."

Several sour expressions looked up at Yargo. "Oh come now, class. If we didn't have school, then I wouldn't get to see you every day."

Yargo stood and peeled off a long sheet of black paper from a roll. She laid it down on the colorful carpet decorated with letters of the alphabet and various items that began with those letters. "Everyone grab your colored chalk, and let's make a big 'Thank You' sign for the Krakun."

Kneeling on the carpet, she drew the words in a big, open style across the banner so that the cubs could fill the letters in. She left lots of extra room for the cubs to draw. "You can put anything on it you wish – anything you're thankful for. And then I'll give it to Commissioner Sarsuk, so he can see how much we all appreciate him."

The cubs descended on the paper with chalk in paw, like predators on wounded prey.

"I'm going to draw the school," Yargo chided her class. "Since I'm thankful for that."

§

Saina stared at Kanti with an incredulous expression. "They visited a society where everyone had huge families," Saina explained. "They had sky-high infant mortality rates, where they only lived into their thirties – and they turned it all upside down overnight. They brought infant mortality down to zero and let everyone live into their hundred and fifties. All without any effort to make us change our family structures, farming efficiencies, or reproductive habits. Of course we overpopulated! That was their plan from the very beginning."

"You don't know that. ..." Kanti was stunned. He feared that Saina might be right, but it ran counter to everything that he had learned as a cub. All of his beliefs were built up on top of that foundation. Trying to break that down now was a lot to ask. "And all the geroo they helped ..." Kanti mumbled.

"Then they show back up, a couple hundred years later ... and they *just happen* to have a hundred starships with them – all custom-designed for geroo – ready to take a million starving **employees** off-world. How convenient, huh?"

"I'm not anyone's slave." Kanti shook his head resolutely. "Maybe the krakun did trick us into working for them. I don't know; that was a very long time ago. But we are employees! I get paid for my work. If I wanted to change jobs, I could. Slaves don't get paid; they can't choose their job! And Tish doesn't stand over us with a whip while we drive our dozers. She drives one too."

Saina shrugged. "You get paid credits that are only worth something within the confines of this ship. Can you leave the ship? And if you did, would those credits be worth anything?"

Kanti threw his paws up in frustration. "Where would you go? In four hundred years, we've never seen another habitable planet. Do you want to catch a lift with the commissioner to Krakuntec? Good luck breathing their air!"

"There are rich geroo up on the upper decks, y'know. If we were truly free, then they wouldn't work. They could just live off of their credits," Saina explained.

"It's a **spaceship**!" Kanti growled at his best friend. "Everyone has to work. That's just the specifics of our situation. And frankly, if 'slavery' means that rich geroo have to do their share, then perhaps it's a lot more fair than 'freedom.'"

Saina was unperturbed. He took a stiff drink of degreaser. "They never even left our system. They just mined asteroids and used the minerals to build generation ships, while they waited for nature to take its course.

"It wasn't even the krakun doing the work to build those ships. It was the geordian. The generation ship that discovered Gerootec was The Jade Statue III. Owned by Planetary

78

Acquisitions, operated by geordian slaves, and overseen by a krakun commissioner."

"*You're* calling them slaves," Kanti said. "Have you ever met a geordian? Do they consider themselves slaves, or are they employees too?"

"Don't get me wrong," Saina explained, ignoring Kanti's retorts. "I don't blame our ancestors at all. I'd have been at the front of the line when Exodus rolled around. Who wouldn't trade sixty years of comfort for a life of starvation and fear?" He shook his head. "But don't fool yourself. The krakun are the most evil, most vile force in the galaxy. They're a ravenous plague."

"Things were terrible at Exodus, of course," Kanti countered. "But life on the ship is still a million times better than it was on Gerootec, even on Visitor Day. Can you imagine what thirty years of living in the iron age would be like? Worried about disease, famine, and freezing to death. Compare that to sixty years of space-age comforts. I'll bet you every credit I've got that driving a dozer is a helluva lot cushier than any job you'd have been stuck with in medieval Gerootec.

"And you don't have any proof that the krakun are malevolent."

"You want proof?" Saina asked. "Okay. What happens when a krakun murders a geroo?"

Kanti lowered his eyes to his mug. "They only execute geroo when we violate the ship's laws."

"No court, no trial, no one ever considers whether the krakun's actions were justified. Does that sound like an employer or a slave owner to you?" Saina sighed. "And if we're not slaves, then why was it sedition for me to say so?"

Saina downed his degreaser and tossed the mug aside. "There's no telling how many millions they murdered with their actions – on Gerootec alone! And for what? Self-preservation? No, just profit. Habitable planets are rare and valuable. So are the slave races that search for them."

Kanti wouldn't look at him.

"Think that's bad? What about all the other planets they've conquered? How many sentient species have they pushed to extinction, just to gather more slaves? People that *we'll help them conquer too*, if we encounter them."

Saina decided that he wasn't ready to stop drinking after all. He was just talking to himself now. "All without ever firing a single weapon."

Chapter 12: The Grotto

The maintenance work on the trinity completed on schedule, and Kanti's air monitor continued to blink blue.

He questioned himself over and over. He knew what he had heard; no doubt existed in his mind. But if oxygen weren't in short supply, then why was the commissioner afraid of losing the ship?

The krakun were one of the smartest races in the galaxy. It would be brash to ignore their concerns!

Kanti decided to share what he had heard with Saina, despite all the uncomfortable questions that it'd evoke about his hobby. He'd discuss it with him after work, when they hung out at the grotto. Keeping it all to himself was just too much of a burden.

"You okay?" he asked Saina as they checked over their green dozers.

Saina's green eyes were droopy and bloodshot. He groaned at Kanti's voice and held his head in his paws.

"Perhaps you need to enjoy trinity maintenance a little less?" Kanti whispered with a grin.

"If you're not going to enjoy the time you have," Saina whispered back, "then you might as well jump into the recycler now."

§

After breaking for lunch, Taskmaster assigned Kanti to recycling aluminum. He gave it little thought, drove to the far side of the bay, and positioned his dozer in front of one of the heaps.

He ducked and stared up through the windshield at the tower of metal above him. Scrap metal was the most dangerous type of heap to recycle. Most of the aluminum scraps in this pile were chunks as small as his fist, but untold, hidden hazards could be buried within the heap: poles, girders, scaffolding. Not only could the long pieces of scrap could make the five-meter-tall heaps come down in sudden, unexpected, and dangerous ways, the tremendous mass of the pile could easily drive any of these shafts through a dozer's sheet metal cab – and the squishy operator inside.

The recycler crew all knew not to dig into the base of a standing heap. Anyone who did took a risk that the heap could topple backward onto the dozer itself. It was always safest to scatter the refuse first and then scoop it back up from the deck.

Kanti raised the dozer's bucket high overhead, and with gritted teeth, he rammed the heap hard. An avalanche of metal bits cascaded down the far side. He backed the dozer carefully up, drove it around to the far side, and loaded his first scoop of aluminum from the jumble strewn across the deck.

He tapped the strand on his shoulder and started a playlist of happy songs to help speed the shift along, but after an hour of transporting scoop after scoop to the recycler's conveyor belt, his assignment hadn't changed. The screen still read only "aluminum."

Kanti parked his dozer and dialed Saina's number. A very tired-looking geroo answered. "I think engineering is starting a new project," Kanti explained. "I've been assigned to recycle aluminum all afternoon."

Saina looked even more miserable. "Please don't recycle the grotto," he begged.

"I'll try not to. I still have a lot of aluminum left at this point." Kanti shrugged. "I'll save that corner heap for last. Perhaps we'll hit their quota before I get to it, but I can't promise anything."

Saina nodded and severed the connection.

Scoop after scoop, Kanti worked around the heap that hid the grotto. One by one, the heaps disappeared as the afternoon progressed.

Too soon, only a single heap of aluminum remained. Taskmaster's display hadn't changed. Kanti looked around, hoping he had missed another heap somewhere.

He checked the time on his strand and groaned. An hour still remained before his shift ended. He had really hoped that if the grotto had to be recycled, someone else would be operating the dozer.

"Oh well," he sighed. "Let's get this over with." Kanti lifted his dozer's bucket high overhead and tensed his sore muscles against the seat belt that held him in place. All of the afternoon's jarring had left him bruised and battered.

Kanti gunned the dozer's engine, and the powerful machine lurched forward, spilling the heap outward.

Kanti saw a flash of green behind the tumbling metal. His heart raced, and time slowed. There, just beyond the fallen heap, sat another dozer. He blinked in disbelief. No one sat at the controls. It was just parked there.

"Saina?" Kanti shouted. He punched the emergency exit button and left the cab without even waiting for the all clear from Taskmaster. "Saina? Are you there? Can you hear me?"

The work floor was quiet. No other dozers operated close by.

Kanti peeled the strand from his shoulder and punched Saina's number into its face. "Please pick up," he whispered. "Please be somewhere else."

It beeped, but no one answered. Kanti could hear another beeping sound coming from somewhere in front of him. "Oh, please no!" he gasped.

He dropped his communicator and dove head first into the heap of scrap, flinging little bits of metal left and right as he tried to dig down to the source of the beeping.

The call soon rolled over to voice mail, but by then Kanti had already zeroed in on where he needed to dig. He pulled his paws back, momentarily stunned at the blood on his pads. It took a few seconds to realize that he hadn't cut himself.

He had found Saina.

Kanti reached for his strand, but it wasn't in its holster on his shoulder. He went back to digging and grabbed Saina's as soon as it was exposed. The casing was deeply scratched now, but it still appeared functional.

He hit "0" repeatedly. "Come on, come on, please pick up," he whispered.

An older female appeared on the screen. Greying fur lined her eyes and mouth. "Emergency," she said simply.

"My friend! He's trapped! Under a pile of scrap metal!" Kanti shouted, not realizing that he was out of breath.

"Okay, I'm sending help now. Can you point the strand at your friend so I can see where he is?"

Kanti flipped the device around and tried to hold it steady on Saina. He hadn't really looked at him since the accident. It didn't look good. He wasn't moving. He wasn't breathing.

"Can you pan up a bit, so I can see more of the pile?" she asked, and he obeyed.

There was a long pause.

Kanti turned the device back around and looked at the emergency operator. "What should I do?"

The older geroo bit her lip for a moment before speaking. "Help is on the way. Can you safely check for a pulse? I need you to retreat to a safe distance as soon as possible. I don't want you to get hurt if more of that pile collapses."

"I have to help him!" Kanti shouted, but he could already see it in her expression. She had given up hope that Saina could be saved. He dove back in. Kanti searched for a pulse in Saina's neck. He found no signs of life. No breathing, no heartbeat, no movement.

Kanti collapsed in on himself. The operator didn't need to ask.

"Sir, please retreat to a safe distance. I need you to get yourself safe."

Part II
Chapter 13: The Investigation

Tish drove up in a truck to find Kanti catatonic, sitting in front of the partially collapsed heap with strand in paw.

"Are you okay?" she shouted at him. He couldn't take his eyes off of the body. He managed a weak shrug.

Tish grimaced at the sight and quickly pulled herself away. She looked at the dozers. "You were operating this one? The one that toppled the heap?"

Kanti glanced up momentarily to see where she pointed. He nodded half-heartedly.

"What in the five hells was he doing out of his dozer?" Tish asked out loud, but if talking to Kanti, she didn't wait for an answer. She jogged over to the other dozer.

"It's in shutdown now, since you declared an emergency in yours. ..." She tapped repeatedly on the Taskmaster screen. "The log says he never declared an emergency. He never got authorization to vacate."

Tish jumped out of the dozer and kicked a piece of scrap with her boot, sending it flying. "How many times do I have to tell you guys?" she shouted. "I don't care if you want to piss on a heap of trash, but don't ever get out without hitting the emergency button!"

Tish preferred that everyone would drive back to the blue deck to use the bathrooms there, but she didn't really care if someone wanted to save himself a few minutes.

Uncivilized behavior, of course, but it wasn't as if a little urine could make the recycler bay smell any worse.

Tish took the strand from Kanti's paw. "Thank you. I've got this," she said into it. She broke the connection and pushed the communicator back into the holster on Kanti's shoulder. She helped him to his feet and turned him away from the carnage. "It's okay, Saina. It wasn't your fault. You couldn't have known he was there. You couldn't have prevented it."

Kanti tried to say something, but it came out as just a mumbled sound. Tish put her paws on his shoulders. "Go home. Please go home. Take tomorrow off. You need to get your wits together before I'll let you come back, okay?"

He looked up at her a moment, but he was in too much of a fog to do more than nod. He tried to walk away, but she wouldn't let him. "Do you have family? You shouldn't be alone like this."

He shook his head. "They're dead," was all he could manage. Kanti looked at her, but he wasn't really seeing anything.

She sank into herself for a moment and then wrapped her muscular arms around him. He just stood there, slumped awkwardly against her bony chest. He'd never been hugged by his boss before. "I'm so sorry," she whispered. "We all liked him, but I know that you two were especially close. ..."

Tish sniffled back a tear. "Damn it. I'm going to be writing reports for a few hours, or I'd ..."

She looked him in the face and waited for his eyes to focus on her. "I'll call you in the morning, check in on you, okay?" She looked for a sign of comprehension. "Can you keep it together, please?"

Kanti nodded non-committally, and she drove him to the huge door exiting Recycler Bay Two.

§

Kanti wandered slowly back to his dreary apartment. He punched in his access code, but the lock didn't click. He tried again, but the door refused to unlock. "What now?" he grumbled.

Kanti pulled the strand from its holster and stared at the deep scratches in Saina's case. He closed his eyes and buried his face in his paws. With a deep sigh, he turned to walk back to the recycler before freezing in place.

Oh no! By now Tish will have reported that Kanti died, not Saina. It's too late to switch back!

His mind raced. Even if he did explain the deception to Tish, an administrator would wonder why Kanti's name wasn't on the crew roster. Nothing could stop the investigation now.

He could never be Kanti again without facing the consequences.

He sank back against the locked door. Now he'd truly lost everything: his only friend, his apartment, his identity, and even his precious bag. He tried to think of a way to break into the apartment, but came up blank. Kanti was dead, now and forever. No one could help him get in. No one could know that he was still alive.

Kanti walked briskly away from the apartment, nervous that someone might see him. He tried to assess what he still had left ... good work boots, a cheap, plastic bracelet on his tail, a necklace of knotted cord, and ... Saina's strand! His identity! His life! His apartment!

Kanti's heart sank into his stomach. Could he really steal Saina's identity? It wouldn't harm his friend, of course, but it was so ... wrong; so against his upbringing. But on the other paw, how could he not? Wouldn't Saina want that? He was Saina's best friend, after all, and undeniably in need.

—————— § ——————

Kanti rang the bell on apartment 719. No one answered. He didn't think that Saina lived with anyone, but he had never actually said that he didn't. Kanti rang the bell once more before punching 15113 into the strand. The door clicked open.

He had never seen Saina's apartment before. It was very nice, he guessed. No one was home, and that was what was important. He dimmed the lights and lay down on the couch.

The weight of the ship collapsed in on him. Saina's death was all his fault. Kanti should have known - or at least suspected - that Saina might be at the still.

He replayed the moments over and over again in his mind, torturing himself.

Why, why, why was Saina in the grotto? The question orbited around his mind. *Why would he do something so stupid? Could he still have been drunk from the night before?*

Saina had been upset about losing the grotto, of course, but why would it matter so much? The grotto hadn't been his only escape. He loved to go drinking in the markets, to stay up late and dance with the females he met there. He didn't need the privacy it afforded him. He didn't need the still.

Kanti had grown up in the belly of the White Flower II. Working at the recycler was the only life he knew. But Saina had lived and worked with the rich and powerful. He had fallen so far, so quickly. *Could that be why the grotto mattered so? Was the thought of losing one more thing unbearable?*

Kanti didn't think that Saina had wanted to die, but perhaps he had been so disappointed in his life that he didn't treasure it the way he should have.

§

Tish turned away from the gruesome scene. An hour had passed since she first arrived at the accident site, but it was no easier to view now than it had been when she had first pulled up. She focused instead on the two males who had come to investigate. The square one with the fiery-red pelt asked most of the questions.

"I figure that Kanti must have left his dozer - you can see that it's parked over there - and come over here to relieve himself. I've warned the crew a million times to hit the emergency button before setting boot on the orange deck, but there's no record that he did," Tish explained. "There's no way that Saina could have known that his friend was standing there when he pushed the heap over."

The red-furred figure nodded. He had introduced himself as Officer A'hee, but Tish recognized the name - if not his face - as the chief of security. "In your estimation, did Kanti seem skilled with computers?"

Tish blinked and stood silently for a while. "No, not particularly. Why?"

"What about any of his friends? You mentioned Saina - does he seem to be the 'hacker' type?"

Tish's brow furrowed deeply. "Sir, I've got a great crew. I wouldn't trade them for the entire ship, but they drive dozers for a living. Several of them could be decent mechanics, if they applied themselves. But computers? If any of them had a talent with computers, I really doubt they'd be working in the recycler bay."

Officer A'hee nodded his thick, red mane. "Did he ever mention a doctor, perhaps?"

Tish looked back and forth between the two, trying to determine whether they were playing some sort of sick joke on her. "He's dead, sir. I don't think that even krakun medical technology. ..."

"Yes, ma'am, I understand that, but do you know if he had a family doctor that he saw?"

Tish stamped her boot in frustration. "I've never been involved in a death investigation before, so excuse me if I seem naïve, but what the hells kind of questions are these?"

"Ma'am, we're not here to investigate Kanti's death. You see, all of our records about Kanti are ..." He glanced over to the black-furred male. "Well, frankly they're all screwed up. None of the information we have on him makes any sense at all. What we're trying to figure out is how this happened."

Tish shrugged. "A computer glitch? Did you ask the tech guys?"

A'hee frowned at her presumption. "Yes, ma'am, they're researching into this too. But if it wasn't a glitch; if someone changed his records – either intentionally or accidentally – we *really* need to know who."

Tish turned to the black-furred male. He needed no introduction, and had not offered one. "You're investigating a glitch in his records?" She tried not to stare at his eyepatch. "But with all respects, Captain, who cares? This seems like an awful minor thing, considering. ..."

Ateri gruffed in annoyance. "I couldn't agree more." He took her gently by the arm and walked with her a few paces before he started explaining. "The last thing I really want to do is waste my time trying to straighten out a dead crewman's records. If it were up to me, I'd let the tech guys sort it out, and I wouldn't give it another thought. But – have you ever met the commissioner?" the captain asked.

Tish shook her head. Few aboard the ship had.

"Screwed up records is, unfortunately, one of the commissioner's hot-buttons." He sighed. "Supernova hot, I'm afraid.

"Commissioner Sarsuk returns in six days."

"Six days?" Tish asked. "Doesn't he usually visit twice a month?"

Ateri was silent a while before nodding, the grimmest expression covering his face. "Sarsuk hates it when anything messes with his schedule. He must be really concerned to bump up our next inspection. As it stands, we have six days to not only figure out how these records got messed up, but to fix them and ..." He lowered his voice conspiratorially, "Well, frankly, to bury this error so deeply that the commissioner never notices that there was an error in the first place."

Tish turned to look at the captain. A dashing, older male with a presence that commanded the attention of everyone around him, there was something about the confident way that he held himself, the decisive manner of his speech, and the sparkle in his remaining eye. Even with the eyepatch, he was quite attractive.

"It's just a glitch." Tish shrugged, still in disbelief that such a minor issue required the captain's personal attention.

"No doubt, but the commissioner took special care on this last visit to remind me that I've run out of second chances with him and that he will gladly toss me in the recycler himself if I can't adequately perform my duties."

For a geroo discussing his own mortality, Captain Ateri seemed very nonchalant to Tish. She wondered if that was part of his charm.

"I'm not eager to take that final voyage just yet, so if you can think of any other details about Kanti or his associates that might aid this investigation, I'd really appreciate it."

Chapter 14: Dinner With Chendra

The strand rang multiple times. Kanti considered answering it, but couldn't manage it. He felt bad enough about stealing Saina's life – he wasn't ready to start handling his calls too.

Eventually, the doorbell rang. He shuffled across the room and pulled it open without thinking. A beautiful female with a concerned look on her face stood beyond the threshold. He looked at her smooth brown fur, her small ears, her brown eyes, trying to remember where he had seen her before.

He blinked in surprise. She had called Saina two days prior! Chendra, the female who made it so very hard for him to think. She looked even more beautiful in person than she had on video.

"What's wrong?" she gasped. She wrapped her soft arms around him, and he fell deeply into the embrace.

He began to cry, and the bulkhead burst open. Soon he wailed, shook, and clung to her as if the deck had collapsed underneath his feet.

She held him close and rocked him slightly in her arms, her furry cheek pressed to his forehead. She didn't shush him. She ignored the neighbors when they peeked out of their doors to investigate the commotion. She let him get it all out before leading him inside, back to the couch.

After sitting with him for many long minutes, she excused herself to the kitchen to make a hushed call.

"Oh, Mom, he looks so awful," she whispered, holding the door open slightly so she could peek in on him. "He looks as if he hasn't eaten in years. I barely even recognized him."

The older geroo on the screen made a foul face. "So again, he's not coming over. ..."

"Of course he is," Chendra whispered. "But there's been some sort of terrible accident. His best friend was killed, and he's blaming himself."

"Well maybe he needs to be alone. ..."

"Mother!" Chendra hissed. "What he *needs* is to be surrounded by those who love him." She took a deep breath to compose herself. "Eat something if you need to, and I'll bring him by just as soon as I can.

"And you and Dad better be on your best behavior, or so help me, I'll never forgive either of you!"

Chendra's mother looked indignant. "I won't start anything if he won't."

Chendra looked back at the figure on the couch. "Mom, I'll be amazed if we get a word out of him."

§

In time, Chendra guided Kanti up to level five and into a luxurious apartment that he barely noticed. She sat him down at a long glass and metal table and set dinner in front of him. The thick, copper plate contained some slices of meat drenched in dark gravy. A selection of starchy vegetables surrounded it.

"It's gotten cold, I'm afraid," her soft voice whispered in his ear, "but I expected you sooner." She put a glass of wine out for him too.

"Thank you," he whispered.

Kanti set Saina's strand on the table and noticed that they weren't alone. An older male and female sat far across the table. He cleared his throat and mumbled, "Hello."

There was a long and awkward pause. The male finally responded. "Hello, Saina."

Kanti nodded to himself. *Right, Saina. Saina.* He had to pretend he was Saina, somehow. Chendra seemed to believe, but how well did these two know Saina? The less he said, the better off he'd be. He was sure of that.

He felt odd staring at the food, so he sliced a bit and put it in his mouth. It was very tender, very flavorful. On any other day, he'd have loved it.

The old couple didn't have plates. The female wrinkled her muzzle at Kanti's aroma. He had only loaded organics for a little while that morning, but apparently he had done so long enough for the stench to stick to his fur.

Eventually the male spoke again. "It's been a long time. I heard that you've been working on twenty-five, in the recycler. ..." He searched for something to say. "Pretty stinky in there, isn't it?"

"Daddy!" Chendra hissed as she dropped her knife. It clattered against the glass table.

The old male shrugged defensively at his daughter.

Kanti nodded slowly, his face an emotionless mask. He put his cutlery down gently. "It is," he replied quietly. "There are giant heaps of food waste down there, just sitting out in the open. It can sit there for quite a long time before it gets recycled. Doesn't smell good." He shrugged. "You get used to it, eventually."

"So, then why don't they just put it all in the recycler right away? Instead of letting it sit there?"

Kanti nodded again. "Everyone asks that when they join the crew. The boss tells them about all the different molecules that the organics get broken into and that storing large quantities of some of them is hard. They tell them that if the other departments make bad predictions about how much they need of this or that, then they'll just have to recycle it all over again to make what they do need.

"It's a very long talk." Kanti sighed deeply. "No one ever asks twice."

The old male laughed and banged his paw on the table, jingling the cutlery. Chendra and her mother stared at him, as if his response was highly inappropriate; but after that, the mood around the table did lighten a bit.

Charl, Chendra's father, told them about his day. Despite his age, he was a lively geroo, full of energy and enthusiasm. Kanti couldn't tell what he did for a living, but from the conversation, his job involved telling others what to do. Kanti was just thankful that he was no longer the focus of everyone's attention.

Marga, Chendra's mother, said less. She chided her mate about his behavior and told him that she didn't think he was being very nice to his employees. To Kanti, Charl seemed immune to her words or at least deaf to them. Of the two, Marga seemed far less comfortable to be present. She shared nothing about herself, but at least she reacted to what was said around her.

Chendra continued to amaze Kanti. She was the most intelligent person whom Kanti had ever met. Chendra was a physicist and studied the universe itself.

Kanti hadn't even realized that such a thing was a job. As a cub, he had learned that the krakun gave science to the geroo and presumed that nothing more remained to be discovered.

Apparently, that wasn't the case. The krakun taught the geroo enough science to operate a generation ship, but little more, hoarding the rest of their vast knowledge. Geroo like Chendra were hard at work to unravel the rest. She studied the trinity and worked to understand just how it did such amazing things.

If the geroo were ever to break free of the krakun, Kanti could tell it'd be from the efforts of geroo like Chendra.

Throughout dinner, Chendra smiled at Kanti. That, more than anything else, helped him rise above the pain. He hadn't forgotten about Saina, about his anger at him – and at himself as well. How could he ever? But he appreciated stepping away from it for a couple of hours, and setting the hurt aside.

Chendra was a beacon, chasing away the darkness that threatened to crush Kanti.

Eventually, Chendra's parents excused themselves and went home. They were very polite, though a little stiff.

Kanti started to gather his dirty dishes, but Chendra put her warm paw over his own. "Don't worry about those," she said. "Let me walk you home."

She took him by the paw, and they walked down the spiral ramp, back to level seven. "Thank you so much for coming tonight," Chendra said. "You just don't know how much it means to me."

She took a deep breath. "I'm sure you had your reasons to walk away from it all. To change jobs ... to break away from how you were living. But I never stopped wanting to be part of your life."

Kanti actually smiled. He squeezed her paw. "I'm glad you're part of my life too," he said. He looked up and saw that they had arrived at Saina's apartment. "This has been a day like no other. I can't even imagine how hard it'd have been to face it alone."

She put her soft arms around him, and they embraced for several long minutes. He drank in the comforting, musky smell of her fur. Her arms felt like a protective shell, a shelter from all of the day's horror.

More than anything, he wanted her to stay, to come inside with him and never leave his side. He tried to find his voice, to find the words to ask her in.

"I love you, Chendra," he whispered, surprising himself.

She squeezed him tighter. "I love you too," she whispered back. She pulled slightly away so that their muzzles almost touched. She held his paws in hers. "Do you remember when we were cubs? How I'd follow you around?"

Her eyes disappeared into dark crescents when she smiled. It tugged on his heart. He wanted to kiss her so much, and could think of nothing else; her lips were so close to his. He could feel her warm breath on his nose. He needed only to lean the tiniest bit forward. ...

"I was always so proud of you," she whispered. "I was so proud to have you as my big brother."

Ever so slowly, the smile slid from his ears. A pain formed in his sternum, as if someone had pushed a thick, metal nail between his ribs, straight into his heart.

Chendra said goodbye and walked away.

Kanti entered the apartment and left the door open wide behind him.

Artwork ©2014 Rick Griffin

Chapter 15: A Special Visit

Kanti crashed on Saina's bed for a couple of hours, but the scent of his dead friend distressed him. Searching the bedroom, he found a clean sheet and replaced the bedding.

His dreams upset him. In them, he confessed his real identity to Chendra, but instead of falling in love with him, she recoiled in horror. He awoke, panting, after dreaming that security had dragged him off to the recycler.

"Hello?" a female voice called. "Are you home?"

Kanti looked up just as Tish turned on the light. He cringed and covered his eyes before she could dim the light back down.

"Are you okay?" she asked. "Your door was wide open. I thought perhaps you had gotten robbed."

"Was it?" Kanti groaned and rolled over. He sat up on the side of the bed, head hung low.

"I found your address on your employee records when you didn't answer. I hope you don't mind. ..."

"It didn't ring. ..." Kanti groaned as he picked the strand up from the nightstand. He stared at the deep scratches in Saina's case. "Oh, right. ... I got a new number. Here, update your contact info. ..." He offered it to her, and she tapped her own against it.

She took a photo of him for the entry and he groaned once more.

"That cannot be flattering."

Tish smiled. "I can retake it some other day if you wish."

She turned slowly in circles. "This is the most amazing apartment I've ever seen. I had no idea you lived up on seven!" She whistled quietly to herself. "I upgraded to twenty, a year ago, when I got promoted to supervisor. This place makes mine look like the barracks. I won't even ask ..."

Kanti hung his head in his paws, and Tish sat down beside him. She folded one leg beneath her, so that she could face him.

"I know you're off today, but could you come in before the end of shift?" Tish asked. "The crew never got to throw a Going Away party for Kanti, so we're going to take the Happy Couple out for drinks tonight. I'll call the administrators and find out who got his birth token. They'll want to hear what he was like, and you knew Kanti the best."

Although not generally superstitious, the geroo believed that new souls were tied to Gerootec. By living their lives so far from their home world, souls, too, had to be recycled much like everything else aboard the generation ships. Expectant couples worried, naturally, about whose birth token their cubs inherited. They hoped that their offspring reincarnated someone great or important.

Kanti fretted about describing his best friend to the Happy Couple. He was a great guy, and Kanti had loved him dearly ... but they wouldn't want to hear that Saina was a drunk who worked at the recycler.

"Yeah, of course," Kanti mumbled, clearing his throat. "That sounds great." He tried to sound upbeat, though he felt anything but.

Kanti retreated into his thoughts and stewed in a long, awkward silence. "What do you suppose they'll do about his apartment?" he asked at long last.

"Did he have a nice one?"

"No, not really," Kanti said, feeling ashamed. "He inherited it from his mother, and it's stacked deck to girders with her stuff. He was always trying to save enough money to rent a truck, so he could get everything hauled off to the recycler."

Tish blinked in surprise. "Really? He never struck me as the 'saver' type. He seemed more the sort of geroo who asks for an advance on his paycheck." She looked in Kanti's eyes and drooped her ears. Speaking ill of the dead was definitely taboo. "He never did, but I just mean he seemed more the type who'd blow his credits as soon as he earned them."

The insides of Kanti's ears blushed viciously at the lies he was telling about his best friend. It felt profane, especially when it was Kanti's apartment - Kanti's mess - all along.

Tish, obviously, hadn't noticed. "He should have just borrowed the truck from work. Hells, I bet the crew would've lent a paw too if he needed help."

"Really?" Kanti felt stunned. He had felt such guilt, such burden over the apartment for so long, that it hadn't occurred to him that he could just ask for help.

"Well, sure! We're a team, aren't we? I would've helped out. I bet a lot of the guys would've." She grinned. "Hauling recycling is what we do, after all."

Kanti felt like an idiot; as if the hell he found himself in was all his own making.

"But if he didn't have a family, then I guess the janitorial crew will empty it now, unless he had a will or something." Tish shrugged, and another long silence passed.

If the janitors dumped the apartment contents by the truckload, it'd be unlikely that he'd ever find the bag again. It was surely lost once and for all.

Tish talked quietly, rousing him from his introspection. "You always struck me as more practical, Saina. Someone who saves his credits for the lean times."

He looked up at her and froze when she put her paw on his leg. "I had no idea about your family," she said, "and now with Kanti gone, you must be so alone. ..."

A long, uncomfortable silence stretched between them.

"Y'know, I've always been attracted to you. ..." she whispered.

His eyes popped wide open; his heart hammered in his chest. "Uh, what? I never got that impression at all!" *Was this before or after,* he couldn't help but wonder, *you thought I lived on seven?*

The skin inside her large, rounded ears blushed red, and her grey eyes dilated wide. "Oh, thank goodness," she said. "I always worried that everyone could tell. I don't think the administrators would approve of you dating your boss."

Kanti lowered his head slightly. "Oh right. I guess if I ever got a raise, everyone would think it was because you and I ..."

"Or if you screwed up, and I didn't come down on you with all four paws."

Kanti nodded. His heartbeat thudded dully in his temples. As much as he wished he could be in a relationship with a female, he was a little relieved that he had an excuse not to try. Sooner or later she'd learn the truth about him. He couldn't predict what would happen, but he doubted it'd be anything good. "It's a shame. I don't think I'll ever get promoted to supervisor. Not after yesterday, especially. So, we could never ..."

She cocked her head slightly. "Well, you could always transfer. Second shift is still short."

Kanti nodded his head, lost in thought. "I could. ..."

Tish was already dialing. "Arpa? Ah, you're awake. What do you think about a trade?" she said with a smile.

The jet-black geroo on the screen was nearly invisible, except for his bright yellow eyes and his white teeth. "Sure ting!" he laughed with his thick, gate-side accent. "Wha'choo got, Tish?"

"Saina for Ghaddi."

"Oh yeah!" the black geroo barked. "He's good. Took an extra shift off'a me, bit ago. But y'know Ghaddi still too busted up to work. Prolly gonna' be out anodder week or two. ..."

"That's okay. Here's his contact info." She tapped her strand against the deeply scratched one on the nightstand. "Got it?"

"Yeah, great," he said. "When can he start?"

Tish looked over at a bewildered Kanti. Between losing everything, stealing his best friend's identity, changing shifts, and then the possibility of dating his boss, he wasn't prepared for the speed with which his life was changing. "Tonight?"

"Great! I'll send you Ghaddi's records shortly," Arpa said before disconnecting the line.

Tish turned back to Kanti. "I'm not your boss anymore."

"No." Kanti swallowed hard past a lump in his throat. "I guess you're not."

He stared into her grey eyes a moment and marveled at the tiny flecks of color in her irises before their muzzles met.

Kissing her was both strange and wonderful. He recoiled slightly, shocked at the sensation of having another geroo's tongue in his mouth. Even though he'd seen such kisses in countless videos, he'd never imagined what it'd feel like. He closed his eyes and tilted his head. He didn't pull away a second time.

They lay back against the bed, and she trailed kisses down his chest and stomach. She licked down his length and he moaned in delight.

Tish stood beside the bed and removed the holster from her shoulder. She unclasped the bracelet from her tail and let it fall to the soft rug as well. She smiled down at him, and he sat back up on the edge of the bed.

She was so very tall and muscular that she towered over where he sat. But instead of acting bashful or uneasy about her physical shortcomings, she radiated confidence. He pressed his muzzle to her belly and breathed in her scent.

Despite the last year that he'd known her, he had never smelled her personal aroma. It was light, but not faint – familiar somehow. He thought back to where he had smelled it once before. ...

He recalled a field trip he took as a cub. His class traveled up to the agriculture decks to the endless rows of crops baking under artificial light. An older female dug her paws into the warm, dark soil as he knelt beside her. With her dark pads, she pushed the dirt aside, exposing a newly-sprouting raddi bulb. The shoots were green and white, healthy and eager to grow.

He pressed his soft nose to the bulb and drank in the scents; moist, rich soil, spicy raddi bulb, the warm promise of vitality and new life.

Deep down beneath her fur, that was her scent. He put his paws on her waist and breathed it in some more.

Tish unclasped her necklace and let it fall behind her. She put her claws through the shaggy fur on the back of his neck, smiling at the attention he showed her.

She climbed back into bed, straddling his hips with her knees. Their mouths met once more, and he ran his paws down her sides. Her short fur was so soft.

Tish reached between her legs and took him in her pads. She helped him to enter her, and then they were making love. She rocked her hips slowly against him; her paws cradled his head to her chest. He moved his paws to her hips and urged her on.

It was not as he imagined it'd be, but it was still wonderful.

He closed his eyes and visualized Chendra on top of him, her wide, round hips bobbing in the air. He recalled her musk, her soft voice, and the kindness she showed him. Nothing was really **wrong** with Tish, of course, but was it his fault that his imagination betrayed him?

He lost himself in the moment. "Oh yes," he moaned. "I love you, Chendra."

Tish hissed in anger, and pain flashed through his shoulder as she sank her fangs into him.

Then she was kneeling beside the bed, gathering the possessions she dropped. He knelt with her. "I'm sorry! I'm so sorry! Please don't go."

She stood, and he stood as well. His wet erection pointed at her, looking absurd. She pushed him away and stomped out without getting dressed first. The door slammed hard behind her, and he collapsed back onto the bed.

His shoulder ached, but the blood didn't ooze. The damage she did was negligible.

He doubted that he could say the same.

Artwork ©2015 Rick Griffin

Chapter 16: Disease

Captain Ateri closed the door behind him. The lights were dimmed, and Jakari sat on the bed, crunching loudly on snacks. She was completely engrossed in the screen just beyond the foot of the bed and didn't look up when he entered the apartment.

A female geroo screamed.

"You're not eating bencardo seeds on my side of the bed, are you?"

Jakari made a big show of scooting over to her own side of the bed, making an exaggerated grunt with each motion. She wiped crumbs from her muzzle. "No. ..." she said around a huge mouthful.

Ateri rolled his eyes at her mockery and grumbled as he sat down at the terminal she had left on for him.

"Viral hemorrhagic peritonitis?" he asked.

Jakari nodded without taking her eyes from the screen.

His mouth hung open slightly as he read. "Oh, this is horrible!" He scrolled down. "Ninety percent mortality rate ... ? No known cure ... ? Sexually transmissible ... ?" He put his paw over his muzzle and turned to face his mate, eyes wide.

"Yeah, I know," Jakari replied. "I can't take credit for the text, though. Bata'ho has a gift for the macabre. I'd almost be afraid to sleep with you after reading that entry." She looked up long enough to give him a wink and a smile. "Almost."

"And these photos?" Ateri mumbled, looking back at the terminal.

"Screenshots from *Pallbearers 3*." She gestured at the movie on screen. "The database said that no one on board had watched it in fifty years. I couldn't delete the file, so I marked it as 'censored' to limit who could download it from here on out."

Ateri stifled a chuckle. "This article is two hundred and seventy-nine years old."

Jakari nodded. "Yeah, I made up all the dates. I linked a dozen different articles to this one and deleted the time-stamps on the different edits." She winced slightly as another female gave a blood-curdling scream. "It won't stand up to much scrutiny, but it looks authentic enough that I doubt any male will hesitate if you make getting tested mandatory. Even if they did, I think all the females on board will make their males get tested." She gave Ateri a wink.

"Males only?"

"Paragraph five," she said with a grin. "Bata'ho's an evil genius."

Ateri scrolled back up and read the paragraph out loud. "Only one test currently exists for the virus' presence before the symptoms present. Fortunately, the screening is quick and painless, requiring only a fresh semen sample from the patient. No comparable, early-warning test exists for female geroo."

Ateri laughed. "I really hate tricking the crew, but at least this should make it easy to get a sample from every crew-man."

"You don't think it could backfire?" Jakari glanced up. "That there could be backlash if anyone sees through the ruse?"

Ateri shrugged and paged around the article some more. "There'd definitely be a backlash if we told them the truth," he mumbled. "And I'm really not fond of the idea of doing nothing. We have to be proactive – as long as the risk is reasonable."

Jakari paused the movie. "Do you think the commissioner really might reduce us to a skeleton crew? I don't think I could go on if you were ..."

"No, it'll never happen." Ateri sounded confident, at least. But then again, he was the captain. Being confident was part of the job. "A vial of DNA from each of us is a small price to pay to prepare for the worst, even though we will never need them."

Jakari stared up at nothing. He smiled, having seen her go through her mental checklists before. "All the medical personnel have been briefed. We told them to treat the screening as routine and to reassure the crew that we were only performing the screening out of an abundance of caution.

"The scanner hardware is programmed to return negative results no matter what sample they scan," Jakari continued with a sigh. "If you really want to do this, the order is in one of the windows. It's just awaiting your authorization."

The captain nodded, tapped on the screen a few times, and sent the order ship-wide. Simultaneous beeps sounded from both of their strands as the message was received moments later.

He crawled into bed and wrapped his arms around her. They sat there in silence for a long while, half-expecting a riot to break out in the adjacent corridor, but nothing disturbed the silence.

"So far so good," she whispered.

"Can't undo it now, at least," Ateri replied. "What about the lists?"

"I got one of the gals in software to create an artificial intelligence that could make objective decisions based on the current crew roster and how many crew members must be recycled," Jakari replied. "She rolled into it every factor we could brainstorm up.

"An A.I. will be more ruthless than we can trust ourselves to be," she finished with confidence.

"What gal in software?" Ateri looked panic-stricken, but his mate shushed him with a pink pad to his lips.

"I told her we needed a contingency planner just in case a meteorite ever struck the ship and compromised some of our life support. I said that we created one a hundred years ago, but that no one could find the source code." Jakari smiled. "She had no problem believing that. I think she understood the need to keep the project quiet, so it wouldn't cause needless panic."

Ateri relaxed slightly and their lips met. "I don't know how I'd manage without you," he whispered.

"You couldn't." She grinned wide.

They held each other in silence for a while. Ateri listened to her slow breath. "So ... *Pallbearers 3*?"

"Really not bad, considering," Jakari said, returning her attention to the image frozen on the screen. She tapped her strand to resume the playback. "You see, they tried to recycle this mad scientist who accidentally poisoned himself in his lab, and just before they toss him into the recycler, he comes back to life and starts biting everyone. Everyone who gets bitten dies and reanimates too. Of course."

"Of course." Ateri smirked at the absurd plot. He knew she loved watching horror flicks, but he just didn't see the appeal.

"Should I start it over?" Jakari asked.

"Nah," Ateri replied, reaching for the bowl of bencardo seeds.

Chapter 17: Apologies

Kanti moped in bed for hours, but the morning's tragedy refused to fade into a dream. He forced himself to rise and wander the apartment.

The apartment was a beautiful place and only suffered a little neglect. Dust coated the table, perishables in the refrigerator were overdue for recycling, and some clutter accumulated here and there. But compared to Kanti's apartment on twenty-four, Saina's place could be an operating theater.

Unsure of what to do with his day, Kanti spent a little time cleaning, and in a little over an hour, the place sparkled.

Kanti answered a knock at the door. Chendra's father, Charl, stood at the entryway with a bottle in his paw.

Saina's father, Kanti reminded himself.

"Um ... Dad?" he squeaked meekly.

"I ... I don't think you've ever called me that before," Charl said with a smile. He entered without waiting for an invitation.

"Sir?"

Charl nearly choked in surprise. "Well, I know you've never called me *that* before!" He laughed and offered the bottle to Kanti. The bottle was made of yellow, hand-blown glass was fashioned to look like a bencardo – a sweet, thick-husked, citrus fruit used to make a style of wine that Kanti had never actually tasted.

"I wanted to apologize," Charl explained.

"Apologize ... for ... ?" Kanti stammered.

"When I pair-bonded your mother, I guess I sort of expected that you'd come to love me as she does. It never even crossed my mind that you might resent me – that you might feel that I was replacing your father."

Kanti stared down at the bottle, afraid that the charade would crumble if Saina's father looked him in the eye. He turned and set it down on the counter, wondering if he should offer the old male a glass. Eventually, he decided against it; as much as it might make him feel better, he never drank in the middle of the day.

"When you were moody, growing up ... stubborn ... when you focused more on drinking your fill and chasing tail than worrying about a career ... I suppose I wrote you off as a failure – as a loser." Charl shook his head without meeting Kanti's eyes either. "I continued to pay the rent on this place, of course. Your mother would've skinned me if I even suggested letting you fend completely for yourself.

Kanti breathed a silent sigh of relief. *That's why he doesn't realize that I'm not his son.* It didn't sound like Charl had *ever* been close to Saina. Kanti knew he looked a lot like a skinny version of his best friend, but he certainly didn't smell like him.

"But I had long since given up hoping that one day you might 'grow up.'" He recoiled slightly, as if expecting to get bitten, and then relaxed when Kanti failed to react. "That sounds really terrible. I'm sorry. It was wrong of me to hold you to ... I mean, that I should have had any expectations of how you'd turn out.

"When you left your job, I didn't think much about it. But look at you now!" Charl put his paws on Kanti's shoulders. "You lost all that weight. You cleaned yourself up. You ... If I had even suspected that such a transformation was possible, I'd have ..."

Charl shrugged. Kanti could tell that the old man didn't know how to finish that sentence.

Kanti felt all sorts of conflicted emotions. He felt bad that Saina's relationship with Charl was so rotten. He hated pretending that Saina had become something that he really hadn't. It felt as if he were admitting that Saina was a failure, and that wasn't what he felt at all. Saina held the same job as Kanti, and Kanti didn't think that made *him* a failure.

But in the other paw, it also felt as if he was giving Charl a chance for closure that Saina might never have. And unless he wanted to give up on pretending to be Saina, what choice did he really have?

Kanti took a step forward and wrapped his arms around the old geroo. Charl tensed up for a moment in surprise before returning the embrace.

The scruffy geroo held the old male a long time, breathing in his scent. Charl didn't smell, or even feel, similar to Kanti's own father, but he shared some familiar element – a "fatherly" aura, perhaps?

Kanti thought about the last times that he embraced his own father – not the gentle hugs that he gave him after the accident – but the happy moments that the two had shared. He had always been such a vibrant geroo; quick to laugh, quick to anger. "I missed you," Kanti whispered without even thinking.

The pair pulled quickly apart, and Kanti wiped his eyes as he turned away. The old male didn't bother.

"Could you come over for dinner?" Charl asked. "We have a lot of catching up to do."

Kanti started to accept but then closed his mouth. "I just changed to second shift at work. I start tonight."

"Oh, well you'll still get days off, right?" Charl smiled, and his eyes twinkled.

"Well, sure. I'll get my schedule tonight."

They tapped strands and took each other's photograph.

"And I'd love to meet your girlfriend," Charl added suddenly. "Can you bring her as well?"

The insides of Kanti's ears blushed bright red. A quick cleaning job couldn't hide the lingering scent of sex from a sensitive geroo nose.

"Oh … um … I don't know. …" Kanti stammered. Was it fair to call Tish his girlfriend? Surely not after this morning. "She's really pissed at me."

Charl spread his ears wide in a grin for a long moment without speaking. "I know a guy …" he finally said. "He lives on your deck as well," the old geroo added before putting his arm around Kanti's shoulders and leading him out into the corridor.

The pair walked down a couple of hallways before stopping at a door labeled 737. Charl rang the bell, and a tiny geroo, his thin, orange pelt framed in grey, opened the door. A warm wall of humidity rolled out into the corridor, carrying a wave of strange and wonderful scents with it.

"Ah, my old friend, Charl!" the little geroo exclaimed. He stepped aside and beckoned them both into his apartment.

Kanti had never seen such a sight in all his life. Planters and pots covered every surface, and a multitude of grow lights hung from the girders. Kanti gasped in awe at the infinite variety of flowers that grew in them. The apartment contained every color of the spectrum; an enormous variety of shapes and color patterns were arrayed before him.

In all his years, he had only ever seen a single variety of potted plant for sale in the markets; a drab green, hard-to-kill, and easy-to-grow vine called Papa's heart. Despite the ship's name, much of the ship's crew had never seen her namesake in real life, only in historical photos.

"Jaca, have you met my son, Saina?" Charl said.

"You have a son?" the little geroo squeaked. "Well, I should have known! He looks no different than you did when we first met."

Kanti and Charl's eyes met for a moment, and they shared a private smile that spoke volumes. It was obvious that Jaca's words were nothing but good-natured flattery. "I'm afraid that my boy has hurt his lady-friend's feelings. Do you think you could help him smooth things over?"

Kanti tried to protest. "Hey!" He didn't appreciate the feeling that anyone needed to do something for him, that he needed someone's help.

Jaca tsked in the back of his throat and shook his head. "Oh my, whatever did you say to her?" he asked. But the tiny geroo wasn't focused on Kanti. He picked up a small, curved blade and was now eagerly seeking a specific flower from within the multitudes that surrounded the trio.

"I'd rather not say," Kanti mumbled. His stomach tumbled as his mind replayed the morning's awful events.

Jaca poked his head up from behind a row of sparkly, violet flowers that were so dark that they nearly shone black. "This does sound serious," he muttered. "Aha! That's what I've been looking for."

Kanti walked carefully through the apartment, staring in wonder at the near-infinite variety of plants that surrounded him. "How is it possible ..." he whispered, "that you could have brought so many different plants from Gerootec?"

Jaca yarped a loud laugh and popped up once more. "Do I look over four hundred years old, my dear boy?"

Kanti blushed. "No, of course not, but I've never seen a real flower for sale. How could there be so many?"

"Ten thousand of our ancestors left Gerootec knowing that they'd never return," Jaca explained as he rummaged through the blooms. "Does it surprise you that they'd bring things to remind them of home? My ancestors brought many of these themselves. The rest they shrewdly acquired when the opportunity presented itself."

Jaca worked in silence while Kanti explored, his jaw slack in awe.

"And where does your lady friend work?"

"Recycler Bay Two," Kanti explained. "She's the first shift supervisor."

Charl yarped a laugh and slapped the scruffy geroo on the back. Kanti hadn't even noticed the older male standing behind him. "You're sleeping with your boss?"

"No!" Kanti shouted a little too loudly, worried about who might overhear. "I transferred to second. ..."

Jaca emerged from the flower beds with a few beautiful blooms gathered in one paw. The long stems had been cleanly sliced.

Kanti gasped in shock. "You've ... you've killed them." They were such beautiful, rare, even priceless plants. ... If the denizens of the lower decks knew that these species were even aboard – and then that they were culled so needlessly. ...

Jaca just smiled up at Kanti. "Leave it to me," was all he said.

CHENDRA ATERI JAKARI

Chapter 18: Dirembo Strings

Charl walked Kanti back to Saina's apartment, only to find Chendra standing in front of the door.

"Of all the things I never thought I'd see," Chendra whispered. Kanti and Charl just grinned. "I thought I'd come by and see if Saina would join me for lunch. Now I can invite the both of you!"

Charl shook his head as he glanced at the time on his strand. "I've got to get back. But we'll do dinner soon, right? The eleventh would be perfect, if you can get that evening off."

"I'll see what I can do," Kanti smiled and nodded. "But I'd love to grab some lunch."

——————— § ———————

Kanti sipped at the most wonderful bowl of soup that he had ever enjoyed while Chendra talked about her day. The soup was creamy and warm, with a strange variety of mushrooms and thinly sliced meats that glistened on the surface. After each wonderful bite, he'd breathe out through his nose just to enjoy the soup's peculiar herbal notes.

A female geroo with all-white fur performed on a nearby dais. She dragged a bow across a dirembo's strings for a moment and then plucked a few notes with her claw tips. The tune was hauntingly beautiful. In another setting,

Kanti would've enjoyed hearing her sing, but he was glad that she didn't, as he'd have had to divide his attention.

"We've been poring over the data ever since the last maintenance cycle," Chendra explained, "but it almost seems hopeless." She sighed deeply. "I'm boring you, aren't I?"

Kanti shook his head and gestured with his spoon. "No, not at all. It probably sounds stupid, but I've always been fascinated by the trinity. I tried to read up about it, but … I'm afraid it went right between my ears." He smiled at her, and her dark eyes sparkled.

"What did you mean by the trinity's 'order'? I've never heard anyone mention that before."

"It's just a theory we're experimenting with," Chendra explained. "The ship's generators route power to the drive, so we're calling that the first part of the trinity. The drive disrupts the fabric of space by generating microscopic ripples that the ship floats along."

Kanti dunked the end of his hearty, black bread into the soup without taking his eyes off of Chendra. He nodded to urge her on.

"The disruption doesn't last for more than a few hundred nanoseconds before it collapses into the heart of the recycler. So the recycler seems to be second in the trinity's order. The collapse rips apart all molecular bonds and releases some sort of … ." She shrugged. "We've been calling it a quantum echo, but I'm not certain that it's a fair characterization. Anyhow, whatever it is, it's channeled out of the recycler and into the gate.

"We still don't have the first guess about how the gate functions, but this quantum echo seems to feed it. So that makes the trinity's order: drive, recycler, and then gate."

Kanti nodded and grinned wide. He was so happy to understand any of her work. "So, your team's trying to figure out how to channel the quantum echo somewhere else so that it no longer feeds the gate. Then we could break free of our slavery to the krakun. ...."

Chendra glared at him before glancing around to see if anyone had overheard. He shrank in on himself, realizing his misstep. "Please don't say that word," she whispered. "We don't ever say that. You never know who might hear you."

Chendra sat up straight and cleared her throat. "Our team hopes to *reduce geroo reliance on krakun assistance*."

They shared a private smile.

"But unfortunately," Chendra explained, "even though the trinity appears to operate in that order, there's definitely more to it than that.

"If anything should interfere with the quantum echo before it reaches the gate, then the drive and recycler shut down as well. Just as if you stop recycling matter, that causes the drive and gate to shut down. So although it seems that the drive must be first, no one can see how that can be."

"So the trinity acts like a dirembo string," Kanti said, pleased with himself for understanding a far more technical job than his own. "I get it."

"A string?" Chendra asked. She looked up at the dirembo player on the dais, and then back to Kanti. "I don't follow. ..."

"Well," Kanti explained, as if it were obvious, "you can pluck the string at one end, and the note will travel down to the other end. But if you cut the string at any point, then the note will stop."

Chendra stared at Kanti with her jaw agape for many long moments. She looked almost as if she had been struck across the back of the head. Kanti started to grow worried before she let out a loud gasp. "A vibration of some sort ... a resonant frequency ... a harmonic vibration for the whole trinity!"

Kanti nodded. "Yeah, like that. Perhaps each ship plays a different note. The fleet might make one gigantic chord." He smiled to himself, imagining a space symphony. "Did you try this soup? It's really amazing!"

"This whole time, we've been thinking serially; generator, drive, recycler, gate. Perhaps the generator is more similar to the pump on a laser, and the trinity is a weird, gain medium that operates in three different phases of space∘time. ..."

Chendra leapt to her feet, bouncing in place. Kanti, confused, stood as well. He had no idea what she was talking about. She threw her arms around him and squeezed him tightly. "That's it. That's got to be it!" she squeaked.

Kanti put his arms around her. He pressed his nose to her neck and drank in her delicious, musky scent. It filled him with desire, and he could imagine nothing more than covering her soft body with his own. ...

"I have to go," she squeaked. "Okay, I'll see you later!"

Kanti fell back away from the beautiful geroo, feeling a little dejected. "Is everything okay?"

"Everything is amazing!" she squeaked. "It may take years, or maybe even decades of research to find a component that vibrates at the same frequency as the gate, but it can be done. I *know* it can.

"And when our cubs, or perhaps our cubs' cubs are ..." she lowered her voice conspiratorially, "*free*, it will all be due to your insight."

She pecked a kiss on his cheek. "You may have saved us all, Saina!"

————— § —————

After Chendra left, lunch wasn't the same. The soft, warm, hearty, black bread was just bread. The amazing soup he loved so much was just soup. The hauntingly beautiful dirembo tune was just music.

Kanti felt guilty for desiring Chendra. And the mention of Saina's name propelled him down into a deep blackness full of sadness and anger.

Kanti wandered away from the table, leaving his lunch unfinished.

He roamed the corridors at random, stopping at each access tunnel hatch. He rested his head against the metal, imagining the adventures that waited for him just on the other side.

He missed his freedom.

He missed Saina.

He hated his life.

Chapter 19: Shady Dealings

Kanti entered the recycler bay to find his former workmates assembled in a loose circle around Tish.

"No, I understand that there's an investigation pending," Tish said into her strand. "For the tenth time, I'm not trying to find out any information about Kanti. I just want to know who inherited his birth token."

Kanti couldn't hear the other end of the conversation, but he could see the frustration on her face. Several other workers greeted him with pats on the back or whispered consolation.

"Wait … what?" Stet'ho whispered to Alil. "I thought she said that Kanti died …"

"Yeah," Alil whispered back, "the big guy."

"What? Saina? Saina had the big gut. *That's* Kanti." Stet'ho gestured surreptitiously at the scruffy geroo.

Alil looked back and forth between Kanti and Stet'ho. "No. … Are you sure? Tish always called *him* Saina."

"No, nothing like that," Tish said into her communicator. "We just want to congratulate the Happy Couple and tell them what a great guy Kanti was!"

Tish looked up at Kanti, and a frustrated smile splashed across her ears. She grabbed him by the paw and pulled him close. Several coworkers oohed in surprise.

"Yes, I'm sure," Stet'ho hissed quietly. "I worked with him for years. … Long before Saina ever started here."

Alil shrugged. "Go ask him."

"What? No. ... That would be really weird."

"No, no, you've been *very* helpful," Tish said, rolling her eyes. She punched a pad into the display to disconnect the call.

"I'm sorry guys, but those mewling cubs in records won't tell me who got his token. A policy change, perhaps?" She shrugged to a chorus of boos. "That's all right. It won't stop us from giving him a proper send-off. The first round's on me!"

The assembled crowd cheered.

Tish turned to Kanti. They tilted their heads down as she pressed her forehead close to his. "I'm still really hurt," she whispered, "but those flowers ... were the nicest thing anyone's ever done for me. I have no idea how you managed to get them, but they were so beautiful. ... Something straight out of a fairy tale."

Kanti felt hot and light-headed. He was glad that Tish wasn't angry with him any longer, but now she thought that he was crazy about her. Ugh. How did he feel about her? He hadn't really thought about that.

He tried to think about Chendra. He felt really attracted to her, didn't he? But then again, Chendra thought that Kanti was her brother.

What kind of messed-up relationship did those two siblings have? How could she ever believe that he was Saina? How was it possible that she didn't know that he wasn't her brother? How could her parents not know?

Well, if anything was certain, he was never going to have a chance with Chendra as long as he concealed his true identity – and he didn't dare reveal that.

Kanti felt helpless once more – as if he were standing on the conveyor belt and riding it off to his doom. He looked into Tish's grey eyes. Perhaps she really did find him attractive. That wouldn't be such a terrible thing, would it?

Their lips met briefly and the crowd exploded into a chorus of applause and heckling. Tish spun abruptly about and planted a well-aimed boot in Alil's tail-hole. Alil rewarded her with a shrill "Yipe!"

She grinned fiercely.

"Are you coming with us?" Stet'ho shouted from the crowd.

Kanti glanced up and shook his head. "Can't. I switched to seconds." He smiled at the group, and they smiled back. They appeared to be waiting for … something. "Go drink a glass of cheap wine, and dance with a female that you've never met before. That's what Kanti would've done."

The group cheered.

"Go ask him," Alil whispered again, while rubbing his wounded pride.

"I will." Stet'ho and Alil glanced at their coworkers departing to go get drunk, and then at Kanti and Tish, who shared a quiet moment together. "But not today," Stet'ho whispered before hurrying after the others.

Kanti stole one last kiss from Tish and then headed to his dozer to get to work.

§

Kanti spent the day recycling plastics and getting to know his new coworkers. They were all thrilled to have him on the team, and almost everyone commented on how much easier it was to get the work done now that they weren't so short-staffed.

He liked being appreciated.

Kanti threw himself into the work, distracting himself from all the thoughts that he wasn't ready to address.

At the end of shift, Kanti passed on going out for drinks. It had been a very, very long day.

But instead of hurrying back to deck seven, he found himself lingering on twenty-five, seeking out the shadowy places where most anything could be acquired ... for a price.

Unlike the open markets in the middle of each deck, the black market was distributed across all the shadowy corridors at the edges of deck twenty-five. Little to no merchandise was on display, but most everything one could want was available.

Kanti wandered the halls. He inquired here and there, but without much success. He was on the verge of giving up when he spotted a vendor that had been described by a couple of the black marketeers.

The geroo was small and skinny, and above all, filthy. He looked as if he had crawled out of one of the large machines on the manufacturing deck, only bothering to wipe the engine oil from his paws.

Kanti glanced around, but the filthy geroo stared only at him. "You seem to be the sort of guy who needs something," he grunted. Several of the little geroo's teeth were browning or blackened. His breath was foul.

"Well, um," Kanti mumbled, "I seem to have misplaced some of my work tools."

"Sure, kid," he said, rolling his eyes. "What can I help you find?"

"A wearable, air quality alarm and an engineer's bag ... ?"

The filthy geroo shrugged. "Detectors are tough, no promises. But a bag? Do you mean all those canvas bags that they recycled a year ago? The maintenance guys don't use those anymore."

Kanti was stunned. "They don't?"

The geroo shook his head and popped something in his mouth, savoring a moment to suck on it. Kanti's stomach turned. He'd heard of areca nuts but never actually seen someone take one.

Areca nuts were strictly outlawed. Hardly the most potent drug on board - they caused only mild euphoria - but the nuts stirred an uncontrollable addiction in geroo. With abuse, the drug replaced basic neurotransmitters and became the only way a user could feel happy.

Users would do anything to ensure a steady supply. Addicts stopped working, bathing, and eventually, even eating solid food. In the latter stages of addiction, users cared about nothing but the drug - wasting them away to nothing.

When the nuts could not be found - generally after a large raid by security - addicts were known to poison themselves. They would eat or drink anything that they thought might give them a areca nut-like high.

"I'm sure you meant an engineer's *vest.* Canvas, lots of pockets for tools, big logo on the back." The little geroo tilted his head slightly. "They do have a handle across the shoulder blades so you can carry it like a bag. That must be what you meant, right?"

Kanti nodded excitely. "Yes, exactly. Do you think you could ... have you seen it?"

"Sure, kid. I'll bring it with me tomorrow. But I'll need a ... reward for finding it." The oily geroo crunched loudly on the nut. "A thousand credits."

Kanti nearly choked. "A thousand?!" That was an entire month's pay for working at the recycler. He knew it'd probably be expensive, but how was he ever going to afford that? He figured that he only had thirty or forty credits to his name. ...

His name ... but he had never actually looked to see how many credits were on *Saina's* strand. He was afraid to find out.

Kanti pulled the device from his shoulder and punched in Saina's passcode. With a tap, Saina's balance appeared on the screen: ₡17,844.1. Kanti's heart started beating so hard that he was afraid the black marketeer would hear it. He covered the number quickly with his thumb, only to take a peek at it again a moment later.

Kanti put the unit away and struggled to get his breathing under control. He had never seen so much money in all his life. He was shocked that Saina would just be walking around with that many credits! What if he'd been mugged?

The oily geroo did not appear to notice Kanti's internal struggle, or if he did, he wrote it off as a panic about where he could raise the funds.

"Well, if I borrowed from friends," Kanti explained, "I could maybe raise … three hundred credits?"

"Eight hundred," the little geroo grunted.

"No. No." Kanti shook his head. "I could never manage that. But perhaps four hundred?" He tried to sound pessimistic.

The vendor shook his head. "Can't help ya' kid. Wish I could."

Kanti made a show of walking away, but an oily paw grabbed his arm. Kanti glared at the geroo who let go immediately.

"You seem like a nice kid, I suppose I could probably do it for six hundred."

Kanti crossed his arms. "Five."

"Okay, fine. Five hundred credits." He put out his paw to signify agreement, and Kanti reluctantly touched it.

Chapter 20: Dating

Kanti returned to Saina's apartment to find Tish standing at the door.

"Oh, hi," she gasped. "I was … trying to get up the nerve to ring the bell. I didn't want to wake you."

He gave her a smile. "What are you doing up so late? Don't you have to work in the morning?"

"Yeah, I do. … I just couldn't sleep."

"I hate when that happens." Kanti gave her a quick hug, taking a moment to quietly enjoy the scent of her pelt. Her earthy smell was there, but also traces of wine and smoke.

He punched the code, and the door clicked open. "Was it a fun party?"

Tish shrugged. "Would've been better if you could have made it."

He gave her a big but very tired smile as he took off his boots. "I really don't want to be rude, but I've had the longest –" He tried to think of another word but couldn't manage it; his brain felt fried. "– Just the longest day ever." Kanti went into the bathroom to wash up a bit where the oily geroo had touched him. "And then in the morning I'm supposed to go to the doctor for some silly screening."

"Oh, I read about that," she said, coming closer. "Pretty scary stuff, huh?"

Kanti shrugged. "I don't see how a new disease could get on board the ship, unless the commissioner brought it with him." He was so tired that he didn't notice how closely she shadowed him.

Tish giggled, and Kanti looked up, almost touching noses with her. "What?"

"Just a … dirty thought."

"What? Come on, what?" He tickled her stomach, and she grabbed his wrists.

"Well, supposedly it is a sexually transmitted disease." She covered a grin. "I was imagining how he could have possibly spread it to the crew. …"

"Ew. …" they groaned in unison.

"Yeah, that's one porno I'm not gonna' download," Kanti said with a yawn. He walked to the bedroom and then turned around only to find himself facing her muscular chest. "I've **got** to sleep. I mean it." He stared at her a moment, and Chendra **didn't** cross his mind. "But you could stay if you wanted."

She lowered her face close to his. "If you want me to."

Kanti felt a smile spreading across his ears. "Yeah," he whispered. "I'd like that."

§

Kanti fell asleep with his arm around Tish's waist. Although distracting to try to sleep while feeling aroused, he soon succumbed.

He woke briefly when the alarm on her strand rang.

"I have to go," she whispered, leaving a kiss on his cheek.

"I wish you didn't," he whispered back, half-awake at best. He really meant it. Although the night had been short, it was the best sleep that he could recall. He felt safe lying beside her. He didn't worry about oxygen, or skeleton crews, or being buried by his mother's junk, or Saina, or Saina's family, or … anything.

She hesitated for a moment, considering. "Well, my apartment is 2012D," she said, sitting back down on the bed. "If you wanted, I could unlock it for you."

"I do want," he whispered.

"Okay." She smiled for a moment before a mischievous grin crossed her ears. "Unless of course the screening doesn't go well with the doctor. Then it'd probably be best if you slept in your own bed."

Kanti laughed and closed his eyes. "I swear to you on all of our ancestors, I've never slept with the commissioner."

"Now there is a porno that *I* wouldn't download," she laughed as she closed the door behind her.

§

Kanti surprised Chendra at her laboratory. "Want to grab some lunch?" he asked.

"Yes!" she shouted, face beaming. "Let's go Top Side. There's a great vendor there. He sells the best sausages."

"Top Side?" Kanti stammered. "I don't have a member-ship. ..."

"That's okay," she said, grabbing his paw. "You can be my guest."

Transitioning from an agrarian to a space-faring society had been difficult for the geroo. They desperately missed their connection to nature. Without it, the first couple generations of crew members aboard the White Flower II suffered a host of problems ranging from claustrophobia and general anxiety to a complete inability to function. The medics dubbed the new ailment "space psychosis."

Those who couldn't cope with life away from Gerootec recycled early, without earning any additional birth tokens. Few of them got an opportunity to pass along their genes, and the disorder soon faded into geroo medical history.

To ease the crew's transition, engineering retrofitted an under-utilized observatory positioned above deck one into a park. Over the centuries, they revamped Top Side time and time again, growing it in size and splendor until it occupied an entire deck. At its apex, the crystal-clear dome towered a full fifteen meters above the park.

But a bigger, grander Top Side was not without its costs. And after a few decades, the ship administrators revised the park's usage from "free to all geroo" to a "member-supported" model.

The fee climbed steadily over the years, until membership slipped out of reach for working-class geroo. And what started out as therapy for a homesick crew eventually became conquered territory in the struggle between the haves and the have-nots. During Kanti's lifetime, Deck twenty-five denizens had to give up some basic necessities if they wanted to purchase even a day pass.

Kanti had only been Top Side once before, when Yargo took her class there on a brief field trip.

Kanti and Chendra stepped out of the gravity well and into a room with a huge vine-covered arbor at the far side. Chendra strode purposefully ahead and tapped strands with the older male at the park entrance. Kanti lagged behind, staring in wonder at the sights that lay beyond.

"Great timing," the worker said casually. "It's nearly star-fall."

Chendra dragged Kanti inside, and his wonder became awe. The dome reflected a pale, blue light projected from some concealed location. Fluffy, white clouds drifted by in a carefully orchestrated illusion.

He drew a deep breath, and the array of scents jarred dusty memories from cubhood: grass, trees, soil. He knelt to touch the dirt path with his pads; the path was packed hard from the countless paws that walked here before him. He reached out with a tentative paw and touched the grass beside the path. The shoots were soft, dark green, and dense. Each blade looked different from all the others.

Chendra squatted down beside him, grinning at Kanti's reaction.

"Do you think we could ... walk ... on the grass?" he whispered.

She rotated her ears, grinning like a naughty cub. "Let's," she whispered back. "We'll find someplace private after star-fall."

The pair strolled slowly along. Kanti enjoyed looking at everything. Chendra enjoyed Kanti's wonder.

A variety of trees lined the path. Kanti had to stop and read the plaque posted on each one. "This one's real!" he gasped.

Chendra read over his shoulder. "Some of them are, yeah. Dock workers trade seeds between ships."

Kanti stared at Chendra in disbelief. "How is that possible? No one can leave the ship."

"The way I heard it, some of the crazier gate-siders take turns sneaking on board the commissioner's shuttle when he's in conference with the captain. They hide seeds in the corners and in gaps between panels." Chendra shook her head. "They look for seeds that others have hidden and try to get back out before the air kills them."

Kanti thought back to breathing the sulfurous air mixture outside of Sarsuk's quarters. That would be nothing compared to the air on Sarsuk's shuttle. *What a horrible way to die,* he thought.

The two geroo bought sausages and climbed a small hill to get a better view of their surroundings. Kanti spun this way and that whenever he caught sight of something in his peripheral vision: something scampering up a tree, something swimming in the stream, something flying overhead. The wildlife was all projected, of course, and programmed to trigger when no one was looking directly, but he wanted to enjoy every effect.

A projection of the bright, yellow-green star began to set at one end of the dome. The sky faded to orange, and the air filled with the buzzing of insects and bird songs. Kanti sat and curled his tail closely around him; he held it with both paws as he watched the starfall. "Is that ... really how it looked?" He stole quick glances over at Chendra, afraid to miss a thing. The sky slowly darkened and actual stars started to shine through the dome overhead. "Why wouldn't Gerootec's sky be black all the time?"

She shrugged. "Something to do with having an atmosphere. It's so thick that it scatters photons – makes the starlight look as if it's coming from all directions."

The sky grew dark, and evenly spaced streetlamps lit to illuminate the path.

"Do you like your new shift?" Chendra asked.

Kanti shrugged. "I'm adjusting to it," he explained. "I don't know what to do with my days, just yet. That's why I've been pestering you at lunch. I did my screening this morning, and then I just felt ... lost. Everyone I know is at work or asleep."

"How did the screening go?" She giggled like a cub. "Did you give them your *sample?*"

Kanti stood and brushed dirt from his tail, indignant. "Yes, and it was weird. I don't see why they needed a sample of that, of all things." He crossed his arms and lowered his ears in a frown.

She stood too and walked closely beside him. "Did they use some sort of machine to exact a sample?" Chendra giggled harder.

"No." The insides of Kanti's ears were beginning to heat. He was thankful that the darkness concealed it.

"Did the nurse assist you?"

Kanti shouted "No!" but Chendra laughed too hard to hear it.

"I hope the nurse was cute!"

Kanti growled, nearly snapping at her. He waited to get his anger under control, but her laughter made that difficult. "They just gave me a sample cup and some privacy, if you must know." He stomped off down the path with arms still crossed.

"Oh, I'm sorry I teased you." She tucked her paw in between his arm when she caught back up, encouraging him to hold it. "I'm glad you got screened. I'd hate to lose my big brother, just as soon as we started talking again."

Kanti gave her a reluctant smile and squeezed her paw.

He wondered when she had talked to Saina. *It must have been a long time,* he reasoned, *for her to even bring it up – longer still for her not to remember her own brother's scent.* Kanti had presumed that the stench of organics had masked his own personal scent on the night of the accident, but his fur was clean now, and she stood right beside him.

They walked in silence for a while. A few others also wandered the park, but the area was far from crowded. Chendra casually led him off the side of the path, and he gasped in surprise with the tickle of grass beneath his paws.

"Dad said you're dating someone. Is she nice?" Chendra probed.

Kanti stammered and shrugged. "Yeah, she's great, but I don't really feel as if I know her yet. We just started seeing each other, and we're on different schedules, so it's … hard."

Chendra smiled. "I'd like to meet her."

"*If* it works out." He squatted down slowly in the dark and crossed his legs. She sat beside him. "But I've never even gone out to dinner with her. It's still really early."

"Okay, I won't pry."

"What about you, sis?" He stared up at the stars. Having such an enormous viewport to look out of, with so many stars visible at once, felt strange. "Have you found your mate?"

"No, definitely not," she said, firmly. "I don't think I've managed to go out with the same guy twice - ever. To hells with males. Who needs them? I'm pair-bonded to my work anyhow."

"Don't say that, Chendra. You're an amazing person. The right guy is out there for you somewhere."

"Oh, sure," she chortled and lay back into the grass, staring up at the sky. "But with my luck, he was born on a different ship."

Chapter 21: Hot Dumplings

"Grabba drink wit' us?" Arpa asked Kanti.

"Oh, I don't know." Kanti had thrown himself into his work, keeping busy. But once he had finished, the grief started to weigh him down.

"C'mon, thereza holy-good venda up ona nineteen tha' stay open late," Arpa explained. "Fried dump'ns widda hot sauce become sort'a team tradition."

"Did someone say 'hot dumplings'?" Veni shouted. The striped, orange geroo jogged over from his dozer with an excited expression on his ears. He threw his arms around Kanti and Arpa's shoulders. "Count me in!"

"Yer mizzus gonna' be plenny peeved widda you rollin' in late," Arpa warned Veni. "Female get cranky 'bout time when dey with cub."

"That's no joke," Veni agreed. "But hot dumplings are her weakness. She won't complain while licking hot sauce from her muzzle, and I'll be asleep by the time she's done!"

True to Arpa's word, Kanti agreed that the hot dumplings were "holy-good." The jolly vendor made them dozens at a time and sold little trays of them cheaply. He made a killing on the sweet and sour wine that went so well with them.

Something in the wine quenched the dumplings' burn. But to Kanti's distress, the burning came back as soon as the wine disappeared.

His new coworkers laughed so hard that Arpa actually rolled out of his chair and lay on the deck laughing for several moments. "Shudd'a mentioned that you wanna' eatem slow!"

With the hazing ritual past and the sweet and sour wine lightening his mood, Kanti told his new teammates about the accident. They didn't pry, but the events weighed him down so; he really needed to share. They listened in silence as he described digging through the aluminum and the helplessness he felt. Each of them understood what Kanti went through. They all knew the job could be dangerous, even if it was easy to forget.

When the tale ended, Arpa pointed at Veni with a stern look in his golden eyes. "I seen you piss'n on trash frommatoppa dozer treads."

The orange geroo hung his head slightly. "I didn't get out of my dozer … technically."

"Think you no get mushed by'a trash heap you standin' on da treads?" Arpa huffed. "Yer mizzus break'n yer tail off'n beat you wid it, iff'n I tell her."

Veni smiled as he packed up a basket of hot dumplings to go. "I bet she would! I'll see you tomorrow, guys."

Kanti said his farewells too and then slunk back down to deck twenty-five.

"You're in luck, kid," the little geroo said when he saw Kanti. "I found that vest you lost."

Kanti tried it on and was almost at a loss for words. The vest fit perfectly and had pockets for every tool that he wanted to carry with him. The pockets even fastened closed so that nothing would spill out when he crawled through tunnels. And he was relieved to find that it wasn't even oily and filthy, like the merchant selling it.

"Six hundred credits," the black marketeer said.

Kanti yarped a laugh. "We agreed on five hundred yesterday. Take it or leave it. That's all I brought with me." He wondered how often such a last minute change in price actually did work.

Kanti noted that even when he tried it on, the vendor didn't let go of the handle on the vest's back – until he verified that the money was safely transferred to his strand, that is.

The scruffy geroo practically ran to the up-well before hopping back to deck twenty-four. He had some misgivings about spending Saina's money on something he didn't really need, but the longer he went without exploring the ducts, without getting away from the rest of the crew, the crazier he felt. He just had to have an outlet, or he was certain that he'd go mad.

He still didn't have an air monitor, but the tools Kanti purchased that afternoon fit perfectly in the vest's pockets – even the new cooking mitts, which were certainly not standard issue for maintenance workers.

He spent the rest of the evening exploring without any direction. He simply wandered for hours, occasionally testing his navigational skills by peeking out of a hatch and seeing how close he came to guessing the number of the apartment that he might be opposite of.

Kanti explored the access tunnels that surrounded the drive and the ones that led to the recycler. He'd never seen caution icons that were quite as distressing as the ones on those hatches! The symbols were red and illustrated the shape of a geroo screaming in agony, his lower extremities drifting apart into a fine mist. Kanti shuddered at the thought.

He found no tunnels leading to the gate. Kanti suspected that workers had to don space suits and conduct a spacewalk to do maintenance on it.

When his eyelids began to droop, he emerged from a hatch and looked at the apartment numbers to regain his bearings. He couldn't help but grin when he read the address 2012D. Even if he hadn't done it consciously, some part of him knew where he wanted to be.

Kanti punched the code into the device on his shoulder, and Tish's door clicked open. Inside, the lights were on but dimmed very low.

He spent a moment admiring the apartment. Unlike Saina's, it was small and cozy, but it was clear that she had put a lot of effort into making the place feel homey. Photos lined the shelves and art hung on the walls. Although none burned now, she had arranged small candles here and there. A display screen hung on the wall, facing a couch that was just large enough for two to share.

The bouquet of flowers that Jaca had delivered to Tish at work dominated the center of the coffee table. He was tempted to turn the lights up a bit to see them in their full glory once more. Their delicate aroma mixed well with Tish's earthy musk.

The scents were delightful, like no place that Kanti had ever been before. He could smell the recently cooked meat and bread, and the different fragrant oils in the candles.

Kanti sat down on the floor and removed his boots, worried that he might track dirt around with him. He quietly set his bag and boots next to hers, stationed at the door.

The apartment had no dining area, and the kitchen portion was just one end of the main room. Apart from the front door, there was only one other doorway. He padded quietly over the threshold, trying not to wake her.

"Mmm?" Tish mumbled. "What time is it?"

"It's very late," Kanti whispered back.

She fumbled in the dark and picked up her strand from the nightstand. "Ugh. I have to get up in a bit. What kept you so late?"

Kanti shrugged in the doorway, silhouetted in the dim light. "I've been out walking. Trying to get my head back together again after the accident."

She climbed out of bed. "Did it help?"

"Yeah, I think it might have. I won't kid myself and say that everything is all better now, but maybe some? It's as if I can see some light at the end of the tube. As if maybe everything could be okay again someday. As if perhaps the future could be better than the past." He sighed in frustration. "Does that make any sense?"

"Yeah." She put her arms around him only to recoil again. Tish turned the lights up slowly. "Oh wow, you're filthy."

Kanti nodded. "Yeah, job hazard."

They shared a private smile, and she led him to the bathroom off of the bedroom.

Tish stood behind him and unclasped the bracelet from his tail. It felt very strange to have someone touch him so intimately. He removed his necklace, and she took the holster from his shoulder.

"You're coated with dust," she giggled as she led him into the shower. "What did they have you recycling tonight?"

Kanti coughed nervously. He couldn't exactly tell her that he'd been exploring forbidden portions on the ship. "I don't know. I think they must be renovating some long-unused spaces. Everything I loaded tonight was layered with dust. I've been coughing all night."

"Oh, I'm sorry," she said as she sprayed down his fur. The water turned dark as it swirled down the drain.

Tish started to massage some soap into Kanti's fur.

"I can do this," he whispered. "You should get some sleep."

She just smiled and continued, unabated. Being touched all over was a wonderful experience. She rinsed his pelt and began to laugh. "It's weird seeing you all wet. You hardly seem the same geroo without being all shaggy."

"And it's weird seeing you ..." He struggled to find a word to express the new emotions bubbling up inside him. "Well, with me, I guess."

Their lips met, and they kissed for the longest time. He pulled her closer as the embrace became more passionate. Soon, he dragged the muscular geroo by the paw back to the bedroom and pushed her back onto the bed.

"I'm soaking wet!" she squealed.

He explored her body with his warm, wet tongue and she covered her eyes, moaning happily. "Oh, please don't stop."

They made love for what seemed like hours before he collapsed, completely spent, in the middle of the bed.

Tish planted a very gentle kiss on the side of Kanti's muzzle before leaving for work. His ears wide in a smile, he snored softly when she closed the door quietly behind her.

§

Kanti awoke shortly before it was time to leave for work. He dried his fur and put a little effort into cleaning up the mess that they had made. He put the towels and bed covers into the wash, so they'd be clean before Tish went to bed.

He couldn't help smiling all the way to work. Even the stench of Recycler Bay Two could not dampen his mood.

A hush fell over the first- and second-shift workers as Kanti leaned forward to give Tish a kiss. He stopped and turned to face the black-furred male.

"Can you excuse us for a moment?" Captain Ateri announced as he adjusted his eyepatch. "I need a word with Saina ... alone."

Chapter 22: Crime and Punishment

Kanti recalled the day that the Captain lost his eye ... vividly.

Kanti had been in his late teens. He had showed up for work on time only to find the entire work crew assembled outside the recycler door. He punched his code into his strand, but the door didn't respond.

One of the other team members said that he had called Searjo, their supervisor, and left a message. A couple of Kanti's coworkers decided to go get a drink, but Kanti - like most of the others - needed to earn some credits far more than he wanted to spend them.

"Do we get paid for the time they keep us waiting?" a new hire asked.

With a single sound, everyone's communicator beeped. Kanti glanced at his in shock to see Searjo calling. Kanti had never seen a ship-wide announcement before.

"Can our supervisor make a broadcast?" someone asked. Several geroo shrugged. "I thought only the captain had access. ..."

The display changed and Commissioner Sarsuk's horrifying face filled Kanti's screen. The image trembled with the cameraman. "You will film the entire proceeding, you little vermin," he roared in Krakun, "or my wrath will be as horrible as it is swift!"

"Yes, Commissioner," Searjo's voice replied timidly. The picture swooped down briefly as the supervisor bowed.

The commissioner cleared his throat with a rumble. "Crew of the White Flower II, your captain has betrayed you."

The crew gasped as one.

"In violation of the charter and high law, I've caught Captain Ateri consorting with pirates," Sarsuk bellowed.

"That's not true," the captain calmly replied. The video feed turned to capture three geroo standing shoulder-to-shoulder on the opposite side of the recycler's conveyor belt. Captain Ateri stood ramrod straight in the middle of the trio. First Officer Sur'an trembled slightly to his right, but she stood at attention as well. Aloppa, the engineering chief, stood to Ateri's left. The portly chief stared at his feet and wrung his paws nervously together.

"No acts of piracy were planned or executed," Ateri explained to the camera. "I met with the ringel only to discuss trade."

Kanti and his coworkers looked at one another. They'd never met a ringel before, but then again, the commissioner was the only alien who ever came aboard. Kanti tried to remember if he'd ever seen video of what that species looked like.

"You have nothing to trade with the ringel," the commissioner roared, but the camera remained focused on Ateri. "This vessel is the property of Planetary Acquisitions, Incorporated, as are all of her contents."

"I met with the ringel to trade information," the captain explained. His eyes were steely and his jaw rigid.

Sarsuk wrapped his left claw around Sur'an; the long, curved thumb talon rested its tip against the soft base of her throat. The view on the screen jumped wildly as Sarsuk lifted her to his face. The whites of her eyes flashed briefly in fear.

"First Officer Sur'an, are you responsible for what happens aboard this ship?" Sarsuk asked. His hot breath rustled the long, brown fur that framed her face. Her jawline was hard, her cheeks hollow. She had dealt with other geroos' problems every day of her life, and the work extracted a toll.

"She knew nothing of this meeting," Ateri shouted. "I hid my actions from her and met with the ringel in secret. She had no knowledge of my actions!"

Around him, several of Kanti's coworkers began to pray out loud. The captain was respected by all, but most of the crew felt that they knew the first officer personally. Sur'an made time every day to mingle with the ship's geroo. She ate and drank with them. She made their problems hers.

Sur'an shook her head. Kanti couldn't tell, on such a small screen, whether she cried. "I didn't know. ..." she said, her quiet voice barely registering on the video feed.

"Are you responsible for what happens aboard this ship?" Sarsuk yelled in Krakun.

Sur'an closed her eyes a long time before she nodded.

And then she was gone.

The image on the screen jumped wildly to the huge archway at the other end of the conveyor belt. Commissioner Sarsuk had flung the first officer to the recycler's deep, violet glow; but as evidenced by the bloody mark near the top of the arch, his aim was slightly off. She'd crumpled to the conveyor belt below, her body still twitching. Ever so slowly, the conveyor dragged her away. Her molecules drifted free of one another, out of view.

Several of Kanti's workmates wailed. "No!" another shouted. A lump formed in Kanti's throat, and he felt that he might not be able to draw another breath around it. His eyes watered, and he felt ... helpless.

He had only met Sur'an a couple of times, but he really liked her. She was amicable, caring, and above all, effective.

Her public execution was not only cruel, it was a travesty of justice.

Jonton, the oldest male on the work crew, began to beat on the thick, steel door with his fists. "Open up, you warty bastard!" he shouted. More profanity followed, but Kanti's attention was transfixed on the horrors of the live feed.

The camera view returned to Ateri and Aloppa. The chief engineer quivered uncontrollably, and he tried to fall prostrate, but Ateri's arm around the soft male's shoulders kept him upright.

Sarsuk's claw was in the shot. He pressed the side of the long, curved index talon against the steel conveyor belt, spraying small sparks as the rough, rolling steel mesh abraded the stone-hard talon.

"This pageant is as pointless as it is unjust," Captain Ateri barked up at the commissioner. Kanti wondered if any geroo had ever been brave enough to say such things to a krakun before. "I am the one who met with the ringel. I am the one who kept it covert. If someone must be punished, punish me."

Sarsuk rolled his claw over and let the conveyor belt sharpen the other side. He said nothing.

"Please," Aloppa cried, "I have a mate and a young son. …"

The commissioner snatched the chief up in his right claw, completely encasing the geroo's girth within his fist, so that only Aloppa's head and shoulders were visible.

"The only way that your captain could have met with the pirates would be if they came through the gate to Krakuntec," the commissioner said as he held the engineer in front of his face, "or if the trinity had been shut off. No ship went through the gate, so the trinity was obviously deactivated. Only you, Aloppa, could have deactivated the trinity!"

"It was a regularly scheduled maintenance cycle!" he pleaded. "It had been on the calendar for weeks. I had no way of knowing. ..."

The engineer's words ceased to flow, replaced only with a gasping sound and the snapping of bones.

"Stop this farce immediately!" Ateri shouted from off-screen, trying to stop the commissioner from crushing the geroo to death.

Aloppa coughed up a bright-red mass of blood from his ruptured lungs. The crimson bubble in one nostril contrasted sharply with the deep yellow-green hide on Sarsuk's thumb.

Aloppa's eyes grew glassy and lifeless. The commissioner dropped the crushed body unceremoniously on the conveyor at Ateri's feet.

The captain lowered his head slightly, his expression solemn. The body slowly conveyed out of the image, toward the recycler.

Sarsuk grabbed Ateri. The captain did not react.

"If your meeting with the pirates was so innocent," Sarsuk said, "then why did you go to such lengths to hide it?"

"My actions were covert," Ateri explained, "because krakun laws are demarcated at whim. I didn't want anyone else held responsible should you decide that my meeting was illegal."

Sarsuk snarled at Ateri. "How many of your crew have to suffer before you learn your place, Ateri?"

"I have always, and always will, act in the best interest of my crew. Recycle me if you wish. I only hope that my successor will surpass me."

Kanti saw the gigantic claw go to the captain's left eye, and he had to look away. He only wished he could have blocked out the screams.

When the screaming on the feed and from Kanti's coworkers finally stopped, he opened his eyes again to see Ateri on his knees, both paws plastered to his face. The picture shook badly.

"I recommend that you do not let your doctors clone you a replacement," Sarsuk growled, his jaws hanging over the captain's crouching figure. "Unless you want me to gouge it out as well."

The four panels of the gigantic, steel door began to creak and groan. Sarsuk squeezed through the enormous opening as soon as they stopped moving. He emerged into the crowded corridor without waiting for Kanti and the other geroo to dive out of the way of being crushed.

When the krakun left, the recycler team rushed in and surrounded the wounded captain. They helped him to his feet, but he refused to be carried.

Despite the agony, Ateri walked to sick bay unaided. The recycler crew formed a circle of muscle and bone around him, keeping all well-wishers from delaying him on his way.

Chapter 23: Questioning

Captain Ateri put his paw on Kanti's upper arm. "I understand that you were Kanti's best friend. The accident must have been very hard on you. I'm sorry for your loss."

Kanti hung his head and mumbled some thanks. He appreciated the condolences but wished that everyone could just stop bringing it up. A lump formed in his gut. He knew that he would never be okay again until the memories could fade from the forefront of his mind.

"Kanti lived with his parents, up on twenty-four. Did you ever meet them?" the captain asked.

Kanti's guts twisted into knots. He respected the captain – as every crew member did. He didn't want to lie to Ateri, but he needed to keep the truth from him. "Kanti's parents are dead," he volunteered.

"Yes," the captain nodded, "but did you meet them before they died?"

Kanti's mind flashed, trying to think of a way out of an outright lie. "We only met a few years ago, after they had died."

Ateri stroked the fur on his chin. "I suppose he must have spoken about them often … or perhaps some other family members?"

Kanti shook his head without looking up.

"Friends of the family? His doctor, perhaps?"

Kanti shook his head again, and a silence stretched. The captain clearly expected a response, but Kanti didn't have one to give. "He was quiet, sir."

"Quiet?" Ateri asked.

"Very quiet," Kanti said.

Ateri took his strand out of its holster and scrolled through his notes. "I quote: 'Kanti was a great guy. Always quick to tell a joke or a story.'" He flicked to a new page. "'Kanti was easy to talk to. A lot of fun to be around.'" He flicked at the screen once more, his eye scanning the notes. "'He had a way with the females.'"

Kanti couldn't look away from his boots. No two ways about it, the captain had called his bluff. "I mean, he was quiet ... about his family."

More silence stretched. Kanti couldn't help himself; he looked up.

The captain stared at him with arms crossed. His stern eye did not look happy. "Let's take a walk," he said eventually. He put his arm around Kanti's shoulders.

The pair strolled slowly around the blue zone in silence. After a while, Ateri chuckled and tapped his right cheek. "Takes getting used to, you know – having only one eye. Have to walk on the left ... take the seat on the left. ..." He shrugged. "The price you pay, I guess. ...

"I don't come down here often. Haven't been to the recycler bay in a long time. ..." Ateri sounded lost in thought, talking more to himself than to Kanti. "Bad, bad memories."

"Yeah, I recall," Kanti said. He almost told the captain that he'd been one of the workers to come to his side that day. He barely stifled the words forming in his mouth when he remembered that *Saina* hadn't started at the recycler at that point.

"Do you happen to know what I discussed with the ringel – the 'pirates'?"

Kanti looked over at him, uncomfortable with having the captain leaning on him, as if they were close friends. He desperately wanted to run. He wanted to hide in the ducts and access tunnels where no one would ever find him. "They never said."

"The ringel invented a cloaking device – or so they said. They wanted to trade the design drawings for information from our databanks." Ateri stared off into the distance, remembering. "I was willing to trade, but I wanted to know if it'd work. Hiding from other slave races was one thing, but hiding from the krakun. ... Well, it had to be perfect ... flawless, if we were ever going to pull that one off."

Kanti was surprised that the captain had essentially admitted their slavery to the krakun, but he let it pass without comment.

"They let me bring a junior physicist to the meeting. I demanded to take our most senior scientist, but the ringel were afraid that if we could learn everything that we needed to know during the meeting, then we'd be able to walk away from the negotiations without giving them anything in return."

Ateri's eye sparked. "Oh, she was sharp. Despite her age, she knew just the right questions to ask. It wasn't bad technology. After the ringel's presentation, the two of us debated for almost an hour – first leaning towards the trade and then against it."

Ateri shrugged. "In the end, I decided not to trade. It was just too risky. I've taken a lot of chances with my own hide, and I've even allowed my friends to risk their own, but the crew ... ten thousand geroo. ... I needed to believe. ... I needed confidence to gamble with all of their lives.

"Not real sure how Sarsuk caught us. I've never puzzled that out, but he knew that two of us attended that meeting. He just didn't know who went with me."

Ateri shook his head sadly. "He really wanted to learn that name, but I wouldn't give her up. Even though the cloaking device wasn't perfect, she knew enough. She had asked sufficient questions that she was going to be invaluable to our future research. I couldn't lose her.

"The commissioner guessed Aloppa. He was a logical choice, so it didn't surprise me when Sarsuk executed the engineering chief. But killing Sur'an. ..." A tear formed in the corner of Ateri's eye. "That was my punishment."

Kanti looked over at the captain, shocked by the black male's frankness.

Ateri glanced at the scruffy geroo. "The eye? That hurt. ... Through the trinity," he swore, "did that hurt! But Sarsuk took my eye just as a warning to the crew. Every cycle, geroo pass me in the corridor. They see the patch and think, 'Don't cross the krakun!'" He grunted a very tired laugh.

"But he took Sur'an from me – just to hurt me, to teach me a lesson. We had worked together for so long. ... We were so close. ... She could read me so well that I could glance at her, and she'd know exactly what I'd want done, without either of us speaking."

Ateri wiped at his eye. "Every day, I find myself wondering if I made the right decision." He stopped walking just before the head of the conveyor and stared up at the archway over the recycler. "I wonder if I should have given Chendra up – if I should have let your sister become a bloodstain on that wall."

Kanti gasped at the thought. He imagined her beautiful, broken body lying underneath the archway where the crew last saw Sur'an.

He couldn't imagine Chendra risking her life to meet with pirates. He couldn't imagine the captain protecting a stranger at the cost of his best friend. The scenario was all so unreal, so overwhelming. He wanted the tale to be all lies, but he didn't see how it could be.

Ateri was lost in thought. "Do you know what makes me a good captain?" he asked suddenly.

Kanti looked up at him but didn't respond.

"I'm dedicated, I'm decisive, and I'm willing to make sacrifices for the greater good."

Ateri stepped onto the moving conveyor.

Kanti struggled to get off the belt, but the captain's grip around his shoulders was iron. Ateri grabbed his right wrist with his left paw, just to make sure that the shaggy geroo could not wrangle away.

"What are you trying to hide from me, Saina? Did Kanti tell you something?"

Kanti clawed desperately at Ateri's arm, frantic to escape his grasp.

The belt moved slowly, their rumbling journey toward the violet light, gradual. But despite his struggles to squirm away from the captain, Kanti was no closer to breaking free than he had been initially. "Are you mad? We'll both be killed!" he shrieked.

"I've read your file, Saina," the captain whispered in Kanti's ear. "Five years for sedition? That's the most absurd thing that I've ever heard. You either have some very powerful friends, or some very powerful enemies.

"What did you think you'd do with whatever Kanti told you? Try to drum up revolt, like when you blathered about our slavery?" The captain's eye looked crazed.

Even though Kanti was certain that this was just some elaborate sort of bluff, he panicked. With every meter that he grew closer to the deep, violet glow, he was less capable of rational thought. He **needed** to escape.

"Why are you doing this? Is it just moral outrage at the charade? What are you hoping to accomplish? Motivating the crew to do … what, exactly?" Ateri growled in his ear.

"The crew is easy to motivate, trust me, but without a way out of this trap, what's the point? We can't free ourselves if we're in a panic."

Kanti felt panic, all right. He'd say anything not to be ripped apart in the recycler. But what? And what was so important that the captain would risk his own life? The air started to smell metallic. The recycler's deep, bass hum rattled Kanti's teeth.

The two of them were coming far too close to the point of no return. All Kanti could see in his mind's eye was the red, warning sign of a screaming geroo, drifting into a fine mist.

"Why are you doing this to me?" Kanti whined. "Is it because ... because of the skeleton crew?"

In a flash, Kanti lay on his back beside the moving belt. His head lay nearly inside the archway, and the violet light clouded his vision. Ateri crouched on Kanti's chest. Their noses touched.

The captain's eye was so wide that Kanti could see white on all sides of the golden iris. "He told you ... that?" Now it was the captain's turn to panic. "Answer me!" he shouted, banging the back of Kanti's head against the deck.

Kanti nodded, timidly; unsure of what else to do.

"Where? Where did he hear that?" Ateri screamed in Kanti's face.

"I don't! ... I don't! ... I don't know!" Kanti breathed so fast that he thought he might hyperventilate. He'd gladly tell the captain any lie now. Anything to keep himself out of the recycler. "He said it was ... just a rumor going around!"

Ateri appeared calm once more - deadly calm. "Was there anything else?"

Kanti shook his head wildly, emphatically.

Ateri stood and turned away. He stabbed the face of his communicator with a pad. "It's out," Ateri said. "I don't know *how*, but I tell you, it is out. We're on the cusp of full-scale mutiny if we can't get this contained."

Ateri glanced sternly back at Kanti for a moment to make sure he hadn't moved, then returned to his conversation.

"I want a list of every geroo who searched for 'skeleton crew' in the past four days. Then I want you to do the search yourself. Flag each and every page returned. If anyone pulls up any of those pages before the crisis is over, I need their names alerted to my strand instantly."

Ateri severed the connection and turned back to see Kanti getting to his feet. A well-placed kick into Kanti's stomach dropped him back to the deck, grasping his gut and gasping for breath.

Ateri knelt beside the shaggy geroo and whispered in his ear. "Listen very closely to me, kerrati. You will not discuss what was said here, today – ever. You will never, ever say the words, 'skeleton crew' again. Is that understood?"

Kanti nodded. Tears streamed down his muzzle.

"If you do, I promise that I will find out," Ateri said calmly. "And when I do, I will rip chunks of you out with my bare paws … and toss them into the recycler one by one … until all that remains of you … is your blood in my fur … and your screams in my ears."

Artwork ©2015 Aim Ren

Part III
Chapter 24: Secrets

Kanti opened the door to Saina's apartment and found Tish sitting on the couch, reading her strand.

"How did that meeting with Ateri go?"

Kanti shrugged, unable to express how traumatic it'd been. "It was ... stressful."

Tish scooted over to make room. "Yeah, he asked me a bunch of weird questions right after the accident, too. Was a strange meeting."

Kanti collapsed heavily onto the couch. He was glad it'd been a relatively clean shift, and he wouldn't regret touching the upholstery before taking a shower.

"Oh wow, look at you. You're trembling," she whispered. Tish kissed the wrinkles on his forehead, trying to soothe them away. "It wasn't that bad, was it?"

Kanti shrugged again. "I guess I'm not very good at dealing with authority figures."

She gave him a friendly smile. "You dealt with me okay. Back when I was your supervisor."

"Maybe I just feel overwhelmed with guilt, then."

"Well, you shouldn't. You didn't do anything wrong. Kanti did." She growled in frustration. "Who knows what the heck he was doing out there, anyhow. I looked it up. He was **supposed** to be loading organics. He should have been on the completely opposite side of the bay."

Kanti froze, and Tish stared at him. "What? What's wrong?"

After a few false starts, Kanti finally found his voice. He spoke so quietly that Tish strained to hear. "I ... I know why he was there."

"What? You do? Why?" Her eyes opened wide.

"I ... don't want to tell you," he whispered, wincing.

Tish sat in silence for a while. She held his paws in hers. "I don't think that's true. If you really didn't want to tell me, you wouldn't bring it up."

Kanti threw his head back and forced his eyes shut, squeezing a tear from each. "I don't want you to hate him. ... I don't want you to hate *me*."

She kissed him gently. "I won't hate you. I might get upset, but I won't hate you. I want to understand what happened. I was his boss. This has affected me too. I deserve to know. Just tell me."

Kanti started to cry, and his breath grew ragged as he talked. "He'd set up a little spot to hang out, there behind the last heap of aluminum scrap. He called it 'the grotto'." Kanti wiped his eyes. "We only ever went out there after hours. I had no idea he'd be there during our shift."

Tish's face was emotionless, unreadable, while she sifted her thoughts. "Hang out? What did you do there? Drinking? Drugs?"

"We'd talk there. We'd drink, but no drugs. Never drugs." Kanti swallowed with a dry throat.

"Did you tell the captain this?"

"No, just you," Kanti shook his head. "We never went there during a shift. Never. I really didn't think he would. I knew it was his special spot. I didn't want to be the one to recycle it, but I didn't think he'd be there during work!"

Tish wrapped her arms around him, and Kanti squeezed her close. She was silent a very long time before pulling away. "That is really screwed up. I can't believe you two did that."

Kanti hung his head.

"I need you to promise me that you're never, ever, *ever* going to do something like that again. I mean it. Or this thing that's starting between us – we need to stop it right here." She searched for words. She was so emotional that speaking was hard. "We can't ... I can't ... deal with screwing around. ... Not at work."

"I promise. I swear to you on all of the ancestors." He'd never been so solemn. "It was all his idea. I should have refused. I will never do anything like that, ever again."

She held him once more, and they both trembled a little.

"So you don't hate me?"

"I don't hate you. I don't know what it is I'm feeling, but it's not hatred."

Kanti sank into her arms. He felt safe, as if he was where he belonged. He didn't want to lose Tish. "I've been so worried about how you'd react. I've never really dated anyone before. And I've got ... secrets." He winced. Even admitting that he had secrets was probably not a good idea.

"More ... secrets?" she whispered and looked at his face.

He shrugged and nodded.

Tish stared in his eyes and Kanti could tell that she was trying to read him, trying to decide if she should press him or leave him be, for now.

"Do you murder young females in their sleep?" she finally teased.

"No. ..." Kanti's eyes opened wide in surprise.

"Torture them?"

"No. ..."

"... Rape them?" she whispered, feigning concern.

"No!"

"Well, that's okay, then," she giggled. "I have secrets too, you know. Though they're not so much secrets as just things I haven't told you yet."

"Yeah, well, they're not like these, I'm sure."

Tish put her arms back around Kanti. "Have you ever told anyone your secrets?"

"Well, just one geroo, but he's gone now."

She lowered her eyes and held him in silence a long while. "You can tell me if you want. ..."

Kanti shook his head. "No, I can't. I don't want you to hate me."

"Oh, stop being silly," she shushed him. "Did I hate you for telling me about the grotto? That's just how secrets are. The longer you keep them to yourself, the bigger they seem to grow, until they take on a life of their own. And besides, it's not as if we've been pair-bonded for twenty years. We've only just started seeing each other."

Kanti relaxed a little, at last. He put his arms around her too and breathed in her soft scent.

"Now if you're still keeping them secret from me in twenty years. ..."

He chuckled softly. "What are you doing up?" he whispered. "Can't sleep again?"

"No, I slept this afternoon," she explained, "so I could be up while you were home."

"Oh wow, I didn't mean for you to rearrange your whole schedule for me." Kanti pulled away far enough so that he could see her face.

"Well, you did the same for me, Shaggy," she explained. "Switching to seconds, I mean."

He smiled. "Yeah, I guess I did ... but Shaggy?"

"Yeah, you look like a 'Shaggy.' ..." She grinned at him for a bit and nodded. "Oh, and thanks for unlocking the door for me."

"It's not a problem," he whispered and then mocked concern. "You don't murder young males in their sleep, do you?"

"No. ..." she whispered.

"Torture them?"

Tish grinned evilly for a moment. "No, not really."

"Rape them?"

She put a paw to her chin while she pretended to consider the question. "Oh, you wish!"

Chapter 25: Judgment Day

Kanti explored the gate-side decks with Chendra. They shared something spicy, crunchy, and deep fried for lunch. "Okay, I was wrong," Chendra said after her first bite. "I thought I recognized this when I pointed it out, but I have no idea what it is."

"I haven't had this kind of meat before." Kanti poked at the roll's creamy center with a claw. "What is it?"

"I think it's bean paste," she replied with a shrug. "Or maybe ... cheese?"

Chendra ate the rest of the wrap while Kanti explored the necklaces and bracelets for sale in the gate-side market. He considered replacing his old necklace, but the strange variety available didn't convince him. He suspected that such interesting and colorful creations were too assertive for him.

Although the gate-siders had no reason to stay segregated from the rest of the crew, the geroo who lived around the shuttle dock tended to stick to their own. They nurtured their own subculture, and kept ways that were slightly askew from that of the rest of the crew.

Gate-siders' food tasted spicier and oilier than the meals available elsewhere. They played livelier music that tended to leave both the musicians and the geroo dancing to the strains out of breath after each set.

But what most set the gate-siders apart from the rest of the crew - those they referred to as "the outsiders" - was their open sense of community. Gate-siders tended to live next door to their parents, grandparents, and cousins. They connected their apartments together into huge, labyrinthine complexes, so that families were never really apart. Gate-siders bolted layers of huge hammocks to the walls on the tall deck that hosted the shuttle bay. They lived out in the open, with no doors at all separating them from their neighbors.

Kanti couldn't imagine living without his privacy!

Chendra gasped. "Is that ... what I think it is?" She picked a tiny object up and held it to the light.

"'Tis'!" the old geroo behind the counter laughed. "Be der stone a' Gerootec isself."

"Look at this, Saina!" she said, handing him the pebble. "It's a real rock!"

Kanti rolled the pebble around in his paw. He felt its heft, and his ears drooped. Then with one paw, he set the treasure back in place. With the other paw, he tried to urge Chendra away from the stall. "C'mon, sis, we should go."

"No! I've always wanted a rock." She glared at him with ears out straight.

"It's not a rock." He lowered his voice. "It's just slag. We should go."

"'Tis no slag!" the old vendor growled. "Ya 'cus me try a rob her of credits!"

Kanti put his paws up in a gesture of "I don't want any trouble." He backed away from the vendor but did not change his tone. "Well, yeah. I *know* you're trying to steal her money. This was never on Gerootec; not any more than any of us were."

The vendor yelled a string of gate-sider profanity at Kanti, but he couldn't make out the words. For a moment, he thought that the locals might jump him for starting trouble, but they all seemed content to watch and laugh.

Kanti retreated to an empty table on the far side of the market, where he waited for Chendra to join him. She eventually returned with the pebble mounted in a necklace. Her ears beamed a happy grin.

Kanti shook his head in exasperation. "I've seen plenty of slag at the recycler. If it were really a rock, it would be in a safe, or in a display case somewhere on the upper decks. Not for sale at the shuttle dock."

"I suppose," she said with a shrug. His words did not appear to dampen her mood. "But there are worse things than taking a little happiness from an illusion."

Kanti thought back on their visit Top Side. He had enjoyed the illusions, too – the fake trees, the projected animals, the insect noises, the bird songs – even though he knew they weren't real. And he enjoyed his illusion of freedom too. ...

She pecked a kiss on the side of his muzzle. "Thanks for looking out for me. Besides, he dropped the price way down after you made such a scene."

Kanti stared at Chendra as she put the necklace on. She was a lot feistier than he gave her credit for. He tried to imagine her meeting with the ringel, though, and still couldn't picture it.

He thought back on Judgment Day – when the commissioner punished the ship's senior staff, instead of Chendra.

Kanti visualized Sarsuk interrogating Chendra instead of Sur'an. He imagined that the krakun flung Chendra to her death, and he recoiled from the thought in horror. He was surprised to notice a new feeling stirring inside his chest.

He realized that he felt concern over her safety, as if she really were the sister that he never had growing up.

"You seem lost in thought." Chendra smiled at him, patting down her new necklace. "What are you thinking about?"

"Oh, something morbid, I'm afraid." He lowered his eyes.

"Oh yeah? What's that?"

"Judgment Day." He frowned and looked for some sort of justification to share with her, since he had promised not to talk of his meeting with Ateri. "I guess since I'm working in Recycler Bay Two now, and that's where it happened." He shrugged.

Now Chendra looked lost in thought. "That was so horrible. ..." she whispered.

Kanti nodded and let her be for a long time before she felt the urge to speak again. They stood up and wandered away from the market, leaving the noise and unfamiliar smells behind.

"Daddy made some big donations to the two Happy Couples after that. You know, the ones who inherited the birth tokens from the first officer and the engineering chief. A lot of geroo from the upper decks did."

"I remember the trinity shut-down that immediately followed Sarsuk's departure," Kanti reminisced quietly. "The captain's mate announced it as soon as the commissioner's ship went through the gate. She didn't even pretend it was for maintenance."

"A cycle of mourning." Chendra nodded, remembering.

"Yeah – that's right. An entire cycle instead of just the seventeen hours that the trinity is usually down." He sighed. "Weird to hear her make the announcement, too. I guess the captain was either in surgery or too doped up on painkillers. ... And then that whole cycle. ... It just felt strange. Everyone drank too hard, stayed up too late, but not like the usual celebration.

"Were we trying to scrub what happened from our memories? I don't know. I don't think anyone aboard had ever seen a public execution before. I know I hadn't."

"I met them – the Couples, I mean. Did you?" Chendra waited for Kanti to shake his head. "So many geroo crowded around them; everyone hurting. I guess we all wanted to see them, to connect with them briefly. The entire crew treated them as if they were heroes, rallied around them. Not as if they had done anything, of course, but I guess we **needed** someone to focus on.

"The Happy Couples marched down the corridors with their strands held high. I think they wanted to deflect the attention away from themselves and onto the birth tokens that they'd been given. Everyone treated them as if they were … well, reincarnations of Sur'an and Aloppa themselves."

"Sur'an and Aloppa." Kanti nodded, remembering that Jakari declared them heroes of the geroo. "Do you suppose life must be hard for them? The cubs born with their tokens? I heard both Couples named the cubs in the officers' honor."

"Sur'am, I think," Chendra said. "They changed the name since both of the cubs were male. And yeah, it has to be strange, with everyone treating you as if you're a hero when you don't deserve it. They must have a very skewed perspective on reality." She seemed lost in her memories.

And then, Chendra started crying. Kanti felt terrible for bringing up the past, and he put his arms around her. She clutched at him, buried her face in his chest, and wailed louder and louder. Several minutes passed before the tears even started to slow.

Kanti rocked her in place and whispered that it'd be all right – as she had done for him only days earlier. Her whimpers echoed in the quiet corridor, and the few passersby kindly gave them space. He kissed the top of her head.

"I was there," she snuffled at long last, when they were alone. "I wasn't supposed to tell anyone. I've been carrying that around with me for years."

"But you weren't in the recycler bay. ... I remember. ..."

"No," she bawled, "I was in the meeting with the ringel! I was there." The tears ebbed, only to start up again moments later.

"Sur'an and Aloppa were so nice to me. I was young and brave, and *so stupid*. I thought it'd be a great adventure and that I could single-handedly save all the geroo from the krakun.

"I was brave right up until I put a paw on the airlock, and then I had the biggest panic attack that anyone has ever had. I couldn't breathe. I couldn't speak. I curled up in a ball like mewling cub and refused to budge. I thought my heart would leap out of my throat.

"But Sur'an and Aloppa helped me. They told me I didn't have to go. They stayed with me and built me back up until I managed the guts to do it."

Chendra cried so hard that she slid out of his arms. Kanti lowered her gently down and sat on the floor beside her.

"Their deaths were my fault! If I hadn't gone, Sarsuk wouldn't have executed them. No one would've had to die!"

"No, that's not right," Kanti whispered, trying to shush her tears. "The captain said that no one knew. That he did it all without their knowledge. It wasn't your fault."

She shook her head. "No, all of the senior staff knew. My boss knew. The engineers knew. This meeting was far too big a thing for any one geroo - even the captain - to do on his own. He just told Sarsuk that he did it himself to try to protect us. He didn't care what the commissioner did to him personally."

Kanti thought about Captain Ateri and wondered how he could be so brave. Kanti didn't think he could face his own personal demise just to protect the others. Even if he wanted to, he remembered how own his body betrayed him during the meeting with Ateri - how he would've done anything to get off that conveyor, how he would've said anything.

"Did you see their faces on the video?" Chendra whimpered. "They were so scared. They looked right at me, asking me why I did it. I still see their faces in my dreams."

"Judgment Day wasn't your fault," he whispered over and over. "Bad things happen sometimes. If you hadn't gone to the meeting, then someone else would've. It wasn't your fault."

Artwork ©2015 Shane Mercer

Chapter 26: Shackles

"Reading the news?" Kanti asked as he entered the apartment.

"Geordian poetry," Tish said with a smile.

Kanti missed a step. "What?"

Tish grinned. "It's a book about the geordian," she explained. "In their culture, they write only poetry for their cubs. The adults have regular fiction and nonfiction. They have poetry too, but the cubs only have poetry."

"That's weird," Kanti said. He knelt down on the floor, avoiding the couch until he'd a chance to take a shower. "Why do they do that?"

Tish smiled and shrugged. "It's their culture. That's their tradition. Sort of like our belief in souls and reincarnation. Other species probably find that weird, y'know?"

"Really?" Kanti never really thought about it. Geroo beliefs felt so obvious that it was difficult for him to understand why anyone would find them weird. "Is it good? The poetry?"

"It's pretty hard to judge. It's all translated into Geroo. The author says that most of the original poems rhyme, but the translated ones don't. And the poems are all about things that are important to the geordian and their cubs, so …" Tish shrugged. "It is really interesting, though. They give you an insight into something that you'd never know otherwise. Hints about the ways that we're similar and how we're different."

Kanti smiled. He loved that he never knew what she'd say next. Just being with Tish was a string of surprises. "So you read a lot of poetry?"

Tish laughed. "No, not really. I prefer fantasy set on Gerootec. I enjoy stories about monsters and magic. I just read nonfiction to keep from getting in a rut. How about you, Shaggy? What do you read?"

Kanti felt stupid and on the spot again. "I don't really read," he mumbled.

"Really? Why not."

Kanti shrugged. "I don't know. Never really liked to. Takes too long, I guess. I can watch a video in an hour."

Tish grinned. "Really? But that's what makes books so great! They last so much longer than a video does."

Kanti shook his head. "No, that's silly. Reading is like work. Would you rather work a short shift or a long one? I'll take the short shift, thank you."

"Oh, you're the one being silly now. Reading is wonderful and enjoyable. Would you rather spend a little time making love or a long time?" She grinned, wickedly.

"Hrmph," Kanti grunted. "I've never read any book that was like making love."

"Well, maybe you've read the wrong books."

Kanti chuckled. "Well, what kind of videos do you enjoy?"

Tish just shrugged. "I don't watch many. What about you?"

Kanti stared at the rug. "Musicals," he muttered.

"Really?" Tish set her strand down to give Kanti her full attention and rested her elbows on her knees. "I never would've guessed that. Why musicals?"

Kanti laughed nervously, and his ears blushed bright red. "I don't know. I guess they're just more … gentle? Real life can be so ... grim, I guess, but in musicals, no matter what the story is about, everyone can stop what they're doing and start singing and dancing ... and ..." He laughed again. "I guess I just wish that real life could be more like a musical."

Tish grinned and stared at Kanti until he got flustered.

"What?" he groaned.

"Nothing," she said with a smile. "I'm just fascinated with what I learn about you, Shaggy."

Kanti hung his head.

"I'll tell you what," she whispered. "Why don't you go take a shower, and then we can cuddle up here on the couch and watch your favorite musical?"

"Yeah?" Kanti's eyes sparkled.

"And then I'm going to download you a copy of my favorite book, and you can read some of that."

He wrinkled his muzzle. "All right," he sighed at last, "but if I hate it, I'm not going to finish it."

"Deal." She smiled at him with a twinkle in her grey eyes. "Now go take a shower. You smell like organics."

§

Kanti stumbled sleepily into the physics lab. He stifled a yawn and waved hello to Chendra.

"Still adjusting to the new schedule?" she asked, looking up from her work.

"Yeah, I'm sleeping some of third shift and some of first. It's the only way I get to see others while they're awake," he explained.

Kanti took some sandwiches out of his bag and set one down in front of Chendra. "Did you break your strand?" he asked.

Chendra finished assembling the device and smiled as she set it down in front of Kanti. "This is my latest project. When you tap the screen, it sends a beacon to engineering, and then it activates a quantum resonator."

Kanti looked at the device and then back up at Chendra. "Looks like a communicator."

She grinned wide. "That's the idea. We really don't want the krakun to find out that we're doing this experiment."

Kanti nodded as he took a bite of his sandwich. It was decent enough; very flavorful meats and cheeses, but a little soggy and messy for his tastes. "I like the sound of that! So, what's the experiment?"

"When we're ready to do the next maintenance cycle on the trinity, I'm going to take this down to the recycler and tap the screen. The engineering chief will shut trinity down half a second later, after he gets the signal." Chendra unwrapped her sandwich. "So for that half a second before it powers down, the resonator will have a chance to interact with the quantum echo the recycler generates."

Kanti shrugged. "Still not following you."

"Hang on a second." She walked over to another lab desk and picked up the musical instrument lying there. "My boss brought his dirembo in when I told him your theory. He's hoping that we'll be inspired by having it here in the lab."

Chendra pinched the top string down to a fret and carefully plucked at it with a claw. The note hung in the silent lab and slowly faded away. "Let's say that this string is the trinity. My hope is that by adding a resonator, it will work as if adding a little more string as it plays."

She plucked at the string again and then slid her pad down a fret. The note faded quickly this time, but before it did, Kanti could hear the pitch drop. Chendra laughed. "It's harder than it looks! But you get the idea."

"So for half a second, trinity will play a different note than it usually plays?"

"Right! That's what we hope will happen, at least." She set the instrument down and picked her sandwich back up. "And during that half a second, we'll have every last piece of test equipment on board focused on the gate to see if there are any changes."

Kanti took another bite and wiped his muzzle with the back of his wrist. "So why half a second?" he asked around a mouthful of food.

Chendra shrugged. "That should be enough time for us to take lots of measurements and photos, but we're hoping that since the gate is shutting down anyhow - a half second later - that the krakun won't notice if anything funny happens."

Kanti stared at her a while. "Funny?"

"Well, sure! No one really knows what will happen. Perhaps the trinity will shut down early? Or maybe nothing will happen at all."

"Okay, but why all the ..." Kanti's eyes lit up with sudden understanding. "You think the krakun watch us ... constantly ... through the gate?"

"Well, of course!" she said. "They'd be crazy not to. The krakun may be a lot of things, but they're not fools."

Kanti stared at her blankly. "I don't understand. You think they'd watch the gate to make sure we don't experiment with it?"

"No, probably not that." Chendra set her sandwich down. "But they'd have to be worried about us deviating from our projected course. What if we used the gate to start scooping up an asteroid belt? We'd probably destroy ourselves in the process, but there are only ten thousand geroo on board."

She looked seriously at Kanti. "But Krakuntec is on the other side of that gate. A meteor bombardment could kill **billions** of krakun. They must have automated systems watching us through the gate - ready to pull the plug if we ever tried to rebel."

Kanti stared down at his paws. The thought was pretty grim. If the krakun ever shut off the gate, then the entire trinity would shut down. They'd be left adrift, unable to use the drive. He felt as if he'd been working all this time without ever noticing the knife held to his throat.

He could do nothing about the krakun, though. So he tried to push despair out of his mind and focus on more cheerful things. "But it could also work, right? Your experiment could …"

Chendra took another bite of her sandwich and grinned wide. "Maybe … just maybe … we'll see the view through the gate change for half a second before trinity shuts down."

"Yeah?"

"It may not shift much, if it shifts at all. But if it does, that will give us our first data point. We may get a lot of insight into how the gate works – insight that we never had before."

Kanti slid to the edge of his seat. "And then we'll be able to turn off the gate while leaving the rest of the trinity online?"

"Perhaps some day," Chendra said, returning her attention to her sandwich. "It takes a lot of data points before you can make a theory, and a lot of theories before you can apply one.

"This first data point will be us starting to saw at our shackles."

Chapter 27: Souls

Ateri loomed over Jakari's shoulder. "Are we going to be okay?"

She stared at the screen a long time before shrugging. "It's not going away, but it's not an outbreak yet. I still don't see how Saina could have known anything at all."

"He did. I swear it to the ancestors." The captain cursed under his breath and began to pace. "I know what it looks like when someone's hiding something from me. That little kerrati was absolutely panicked that I would find out."

"Well, I'm not seeing how that can be. Only one search for 'skeleton crew' was made recently, and by none other than Kanti himself, shortly before his death." Jakari furrowed her brow and gestured at the screen. "Look at the timestamp! Right after your meeting with the commissioner."

"He knew! He knew somehow." Ateri cracked his knuckles as he paced. "No one else did at that point. Sarsuk hadn't contacted anyone, and I hadn't even told you yet. Could he have bugged the commissioner's chamber, somehow?"

"He drove a dozer and had no traces of a political agenda. It has to have been a coincidence. Kanti searched for 'skeleton crew' and then downloaded a porno by that name." She shrugged again. "I think he was just entertaining himself. If he really had any knowledge of your discussion with Sarsuk, then he didn't act the part. He's a dead end – figuratively and literally."

"A porno about 'skeleton crew'?" Ateri made a foul face. "That's sick!"

Jakari tapped a few keys and brought up the video's blurb. "Eh, it sounds pretty ordinary, actually. Guy finds a skeleton crew ship crewed only by females and then mates with all of them. Not exactly a suspenseful thriller."

"I suppose so, but there's no such thing as coincidence," Ateri grumbled. "Perhaps Kanti didn't know, but Saina *does*. I could see right through him."

The captain collapsed in a seat and turned it to face Jakari. "What if Kanti told Saina about the porno, and then once we ordered the semen collections, Saina put the pieces together?"

"It's possible, I suppose. But whether he worked it out or not, it's very clear that he hasn't told anyone … yet. No one else has done the search. If he had blabbed, then someone else would've, I assure you. This thing would be spreading like a fuel fire – and it's just not."

"So we're safe, then," Ateri said with authority. "Saina is spineless. I put the fear of the five hells into him. If he hadn't said anything before our little one-on-one, then he sure won't say anything after it."

"No, I don't think the danger has passed at all." Jakari turned back to the screen. "All the 'medical screenings' are done, but related searches keep popping up. The medics told every male that he didn't have the disease, and that he shouldn't worry about it, but the crew hasn't let it go yet. There's a distinct surge in search terms such as 'semen samples' and 'cloning'.

"They haven't pieced it together, but there's clearly a sentiment in the crew that we've deceived them. They're looking for the conspiracy theory now. I think we're only safe until someone makes that connection."

"So it all comes down to whether anyone can add it up before the next new distraction comes along?"

"That's my guess." Jakari nodded. "Any ideas?"

Ateri shrugged. "Give them a distraction, wait and hope, or be honest with them. I'm not crazy about any of the options."

Ateri flopped down on the bed, and rubbed his temples. "Sarsuk returns tomorrow, and this mess isn't even close to being cleaned up. No way we can bury it, not at this point."

He took off his eyepatch and set it on the nightstand. "I have a really bad feeling about this upcoming inspection."

§

Veni rubbed Aprisma's swollen belly. "He got a navigator's birth token, so of course we have high hopes."

"May he bring our cubs to a world of their own," Menno said with a smile. "Where they can feel warm starshine on their faces and cool grasses under paw."

"To a colony," the group toasted, holding up their cups of sweet and sour wine.

Kanti hesitated, lost deep in thought.

Finding planets that the **krakun** could colonize was the ship's primary mission, of course. In the past four hundred years, the White Flower II had surveyed dozens of solar systems and hundreds of planets. They had added entries on all of them into the extensive krakun planetary database. But they'd yet to come across a single habitable planet.

Habitable planets were rare jewels. Most planets were too hot, too cold, or massive gas giants. That or they completely lacked an atmosphere. Any number of factors made a planet unable to sustain life. And with a quarter of a trillion star systems in the galaxy, it was anyone's guess where the nearest viable planet might lie.

And even if they found a planet capable of supporting life, no one could guarantee what sort of life that might be.

Geroo couldn't survive on Krakuntec, for instance, or on most of the home-worlds of the Galaxy's other known races.

If they did find a viable world, the planet could have only single-celled organisms on it, or perhaps beings even more advanced than the krakun.

Kanti feared what would happen if they found another race that the krakun could enslave. He didn't want to help do to them what the geordian helped do to the geroo. But what choice would they have?

And what if they did find a planet that the geroo could colonize; a planet that didn't already have a sentient race on it? Would the krakun allow them to stay there? Would they prevent the geroo from abandoning the ship?

Kanti looked around at his cheerful coworkers. Most geroo seemed ever-hopeful that they'd find a new world of their own. But did they truly believe it possible, or was this just a show to keep the others from despair? Did they fear that their servitude to the krakun would be without end?

Regardless, Kanti didn't want to be a creased whisker either. "To a colony," Kanti returned the toast. He forced his ears to smile.

"Nice one!" Tish said. "My dad said that I inherited a token from a farmer who was known as quite a brawler when he was young." She pretended to throw a few punches in the air before popping another hot dumpling in her mouth. "Said he made a lot of credits betting on himself. Dad thought that was why I ended up with such a ..." she rolled her eyes sarcastically, "... girly figure."

Everyone laughed at the joke but Kanti. "Well, *I* think you're gorgeous," he slurred a little when the laughter died down. They shared a peck of a kiss.

"I think you're drunk." Tish grinned.

Kanti shook his head a moment, and then tried to stabilize himself. "I think you're right."

"Me mudda said I get me granmudda's token," Arpa said in his thick, gate-side accent. "How bout dat?"

Everyone oohed simultaneously. "Wow, that's gotta' be rare!" Kanti blurted.

"My neighbor said she got her great-uncle's token," Aprisma interjected. "But that's not nearly as cool as your own grandmother."

Everyone assembled had to agree.

"How about you, Shaggy?" Tish asked. "Whose token did you get?"

Kanti's ears blushed furiously at the nickname. She'd never said it outside of the apartment, and certainly never in front of his friends. "Tish!" he hissed.

Everyone but Kanti got a good laugh. A couple of geroo mocked, "Shaggy!"

"Seriously though, whose token did you get?" Tish repeated.

Kanti felt very conspicuous and wished that everyone would stop staring at him. Because he didn't actually have a birth token, he hadn't inherited one from anyone. He shrugged. "I don't know. My parents ... they never said."

After a brief pause, a few geroo oohed ominously.

"Mebbe it from a criminal?" Arpa interjected. "Or victim a murder?"

Tish punched her former supervisor in the shoulder. "That's a terrible thing to say! Besides, sometimes they just don't tell you. They wouldn't tell me who got Kanti's after the accident."

Several geroo nodded.

"Did you ever look in the records, out of curiosity?" Aprisma asked. "To try to figure out who got recycled around the time you were conceived, I mean?"

Kanti just shrugged. "No, can't say that I ever did."

"That's pretty scary," Veni's mate continued. "What if it really was from a murderer. ... A criminal who got executed? It doesn't happen often, but that could explain why they didn't tell you." She looked very worried. "Maybe you have the soul of a criminal. ..."

"Well, I haven't murdered anyone ..." he grinned drunkenly at Aprisma, "yet."

The others laughed, but Tish scowled angrily at the round geroo. Aprisma had a grey and white coat that was completely white across her wide belly. She was curvy before getting pregnant, but she was a big ball of fur now. "I don't think it works that way," Tish said. "A birth token is nothing. It's a license to breed. My birth token is no more significant than any other file on my strand."

Several others shook their heads. "Gerootec is over fifteen hundred light years away," Veni's mate said. "How could a new soul travel all that way when a geroo is conceived? It couldn't. There are only ten thousand souls on board this ship. You have to have one of them. It's not as if we can make more."

Kanti looked around frantically. His heart raced, and sweat moistened his pads. He panted a little, without even realizing it. What if he really had no soul? He had wondered idly about this when he was sober, but the thought was especially terrifying now. Could the others tell that he was spiritually malformed?

But no one paid any attention to him. Tish waved her arms. "That's absurd. What if we had no such things as birth tokens, and we just bred whenever we wanted?"

"We'd overpopulate," Veni said into his drink.

"Well, of course!" Tish said. "But it's a thought experiment. What if that were the case? What if more geroo were born than died? Do you think the excess geroo would be normal, or do you think they'd be born without souls?"

Everyone in the assembled group looked at each other for a moment in silence.

"Perhap dey get soul da alien world," Arpa said quietly. "Alien soul in geroo bod. Ooh! Magine un krakun soul in geroo bod! Might hate 'imself."

Veni laughed and clapped a paw on Arpa's back.

Tish gruffed loudly and turned to Kanti. "What do you think, Shaggy? Think you might have a tainted soul, just because you don't know who had your birth token before you?"

Everyone stared at Kanti, but for once he was not the least bit embarrassed. He stared at Tish for the longest time and smiled. No matter how he felt about himself, she was always steadfast; believing in him, standing up for him, even when she didn't realize it.

He wondered how he could have worked alongside her for an entire year without ever really noticing her. She was kind, strong, nurturing – he was amazed that he had ignored her before, just because she was tall and muscular. A change was coming over him. He looked for her in every crowd and felt incomplete when she wasn't around.

When he finally spoke, he said, "I think that you're the most amazing female on this ship, Tish. And that if you won't dance with me right now –" He used the geroo euphemism for dropping dead. "– That they'll give my birth token away."

She grabbed Kanti by the paw and led him out to the mostly empty dance floor. "Well, we wouldn't want that," she said just to him.

Chapter 28: An Example

Kanti pressed his nose up against the glass. "Is that the commissioner's shuttle?"

Chendra peered into the bridge from the overlook. "It must be. They're tracking it coming through the gate."

The captain stood at attention with paws folded behind his back. The first officer, communications officer, and four other officers sat at their stations, overseeing the transit.

"He's awful early, isn't he?" Chendra mumbled. "Why do you suppose he's come back so soon?"

Kanti's stomach tumbled. His brain replayed the horrifying encounter with Ateri over and over. The captain was worried about a mutiny, all because Kanti overheard Sarsuk mention "skeleton crew."

The commissioner's early return didn't ease the queasiness in Kanti's stomach.

The shuttle completed its docking procedure, and the captain ordered the shuttle bay sealed and pressurized. Ateri turned to leave the bridge so that he could go greet the commissioner in person, but he paused when he saw Chendra and Kanti staring at him from the windowed overlook.

Kanti wanted to hide himself away. Ateri said nothing. He simply stood there a moment before nodding once at the pair and heading out.

"Did you see that?" Chendra gasped. "I think he still remembers me!"

Kanti thought he might throw up. He put on a smile to cover his nerves and patted her on the back. "How could he not?"

Chendra turned and wandered away, grinning widely. Kanti followed, clutching his guts.

"So, how's it going with your mystery female?" she asked with a wink.

Kanti's ears blushed red. "Good." He struggled to overcome his anxiety and chose to think of Tish instead. "Really good, actually. It's as if she really gets me. As if we're on the same wavelength. And at the same time, we're still really different. She's constantly getting me to try something that I've never tried before."

"Aw, that's great." She put a paw on his shoulder. "You seem really happy."

"I am. I hate to say it, but this could be the first time that I've ever been happy ... truly happy."

"Oh." She stopped and stared at him with eyes wide. "Am I hearing ... what I *think* I'm hearing? Did my brother – my love-them-and-leave-them brother – meet *the one*?"

Kanti shrugged and smiled. "She's been staying at my place. We've been talking about letting her lease lapse at the end of the month."

"Wow ... that was ... quick." Chendra blinked in surprise. "How long have you known her?"

"We haven't been dating long, but we've known each other for a year." Kanti's worry bubbled up again. "Do you think we're moving too fast?"

Chendra smiled. "Oh, hells no. You're happy. What more could you hope for?"

Kanti grinned stupidly. "Thanks, sis. That means a lot coming from you."

His smile faded slowly as he realized how agitated Chendra seemed. It was as if she didn't know what to do with her arms; she crossed them, she put her paws on her hips, she wrung her paws in front of her.

Kanti worried some more. Did she think that Tish moving in with him was a bad idea? Why was she so supportive, if she didn't approve?

"So did you tell her all about our 'crazy family'?" She gestured erratically with her paws.

"It doesn't seem all that crazy to me," Kanti said, but his voice lacked confidence.

"No?" Her expression was blank. "Then why did you cut us all off?"

Kanti stared down at the deck, afraid to meet her gaze. He needed to get out of this conversation. He just didn't know enough about Saina's past to discuss it.

"Until this last week, I hadn't spoken this much to you since we were cubs. I can't even recall when I saw you last. And all because Mom got pair-bonded a second time? It was almost thirty years ago, Saina."

"It doesn't sound as if you're calling the family crazy, sis," he mumbled.

"I didn't mean it like that." She put her paw on his back.

"I can't explain the past." He stared down the corridor. "But I am trying to fix it."

They walked in silence a while, and Kanti was thankful that she let the subject drop. "We could go look at the engine room," Chendra said finally. "If you wanted to."

Kanti shook his head. "The engine room doesn't have an observation deck."

"That's okay. I know most of the engineers. They won't mind." She chewed her lip a moment in thought. "But we should hurry. Sarsuk tours the engine room occasionally. We'll want to finish before he gets settled."

Chendra gave him a quick tour of the engine room. Although the constant him from the generator was not loud, they had to raise their voices.

"Plasma loops through the reactor," Chendra explained. "Hydrogen is combined into helium, and helium into oxygen and carbon. Each fusion liberates energy bound in the atomic nuclei, so the top of the plasma coil is much hotter than the bottom."

They walked along the blue path beside the reactor. Chendra continued, "The hot plasma loops through a symmetric coil in the generator, which converts the excess heat directly into electricity, cooling the plasma back down. The 'cold' plasma is fed back into the bottom of the reactor."

Kanti stared in wide-eyed wonder. His nose twitched as he drank in a hundred different scents.

"It's ozone," Chendra explained. "That sweet, oily smell? The generator leaks a little ozone.

"Do you know what those are?" She gestured to a pair of copper tubes running between the generator and the drive. Each was about as wide around as Chendra, at the waist.

Kanti shrugged. He had always been terrible at science. "Tubes for piping ... the ozone away?"

Chendra grinned. "Those are solid copper bus bars. They're the biggest wires you'll ever see in your life. They deliver power to the drive."

Kanti's head spun in amazement. He had never imagined what any of this looked like. The drive was a toroid that he guessed was about the same size as his apartment. Though the drive was huge, he'd always presumed it was even larger. He certainly hadn't thought about all of the other components necessary to support it.

When they finally left the engine room, he had a big, stupid grin on his ears. He sighed happily. "Thanks, sis," he sighed. "You really made my day!"

Chendra grinned and looked down at the deck.

"I can't believe you actually met the ringel," Kanti blurted as the thought crossed his mind. "What were they like?"

Chendra stared blankly down the corridor, apparently trying to think of words to describe them. "Terrifying. ... Absolutely terrifying. Smart certainly, but it was a complete horror show."

"Really?" Kanti was riveted. "I researched them on the network. I thought they were a little smaller than us. They don't look so fierce in the photos."

"Oh, it's not that, but they're really ... ugh." Chendra struggled for words. "How about 'overtly sexual'? Like ... really ... really ... really ..."

Kanti wasn't expecting that. He recoiled a few centimeters. "Really?"

"Yes. They can't keep their paws off of each other. At all. ... I could tell that Captain Ateri was constantly positioning himself to stay between me and them. It was ... unnerving to say the least.

"Their ship was dimly lit. The rooms were hot and claustrophobic." Her eyes flashed wide, and she wrinkled her muzzle in disgust. "And the ... smell!"

"Stinky?" Kanti's ears showed his concern. "Not as bad as the recycler, I bet."

"It smelled as if they had had ... sex on every surface in the entire ship. It was that strong."

Kanti stared, lost for words. "... Really?"

"Yeah. ..." Chendra whispered, lost in her memories. "I was afraid to touch anything."

Kanti giggled nervously, imagining what it must have been like. The sound roused her from her thoughts, and her ears blushed bright red. She giggled too.

Soon, Kanti and Chendra were both laughing until their sides ached.

———————   §   ———————

Commissioner Sarsuk flicked a claw across the surface of his strand, paging through Ateri's proposed plans. He did not look pleased, but then again, he never did.

Ateri stood stock-still. There was no point in trying to discern the commissioner's opinion – he would hear it soon enough. Besides, moving his head only brought on vertigo.

"I suppose this could work, but I really don't fathom this geroo obsession with subtlety." Sarsuk sighed. "Your crew disobeys you because they don't **fear** you. That's the root of the problem. What I need to do is to put the fear back into them. If they truly fear the repercussions, then they will not dare to defy."

It sounded like a typical krakun solution to a problem, and Ateri worried about the direction Sarsuk was headed. Anything the commissioner did to make the crew fear him more could only spell harm for the crew. "I assure you, Commissioner, the crew is terrified of you."

The commissioner ignored him. "I want you to find the stowaways and execute them publicly. And I don't mean your silly, orange pills. The execution needs to send a message – it needs to be **messy**."

"If the plan I've proposed is acceptable, then I'll implement it immediately." Ateri showed no expression. He sincerely hoped that no more stowaways were found. He wasn't ready to wrestle with the moral dilemmas of a "messy" execution.

Ateri took out his strand and tapped its surface to bring up the proposal. "I personally believe that Kanti was the only anomaly. Our investigations into his background show no larger conspiracy, no shadowy network beyond the census. He was an aberration, an exception. But if we find others, we will deal with them. ..."

"Find me the stowaways, and execute them now."

Stunned and unsure of how to respond, Ateri stuttered, "Now?"

"Well, it doesn't have to be this very instant," Sarsuk replied in Krakun. "I'm not leaving for several hours."

"Sir, you've read the plan I've outlined. I think it can be enacted quite quickly. We might even have results as early as your next visit, but ... within hours ... ?"

"I wish to make an example of someone." Sarsuk hissed a loud sigh as if Ateri were too simple to understand. "*Someone.* If you can't find an actual stowaway, then pick someone else, and declare him illegal. I really don't care."

Ateri had made many sacrifices in the name of the greater good, but a sacrifice just for the sake of making the crew fear? That was simply going too far. "I can't. ..."

"Are you volunteering, Ateri? Is that what I'm hearing?" Sarsuk growled.

"I've told you many times, Commissioner. You can recycle me if you wish." He puffed out his chest. "Since accepting this position, I've had no delusion that I'd receive my full sixty years."

"I find your selflessness positively tedious. Is there no one that I can make an example of?" Sarsuk grinned with far too many meter-long teeth. "How about that little mate of yours. What is her name? Jakari?"

Ateri felt his hatred for the krakun rising from his gut, but he forced it back down. "Recycle her if you wish, but that won't accomplish your goals. She is well-loved by the whole crew. It won't make them fear you. I dare say that you'd be inspiring rebellion."

Sarsuk sighed again and brought his head down close to the captain's face. "You really are tiresome, Ateri. Fine. Bring me that doctor. What was his name? Hitera?"

"Doctor Hitera has already been punished for his crime."

"I'm losing my patience," Sarsuk growled. "Bring him …
now."

Chapter 29: A Date

Kanti stared at the tiles for a moment, trying to recall where he'd seen the seven. He flipped one over. "Red three," he grumbled. "Not what I need." He flipped a second tile face down and then drew a third, sighing as he looked at it. "You know that Veni and his mate invited us over to play this exact same game, right?"

"We hung out with them yesterday." Tish studied the tiles in her paw intently without looking up. "Besides, Aprisma kind of pisses me off."

"Why?" Kanti asked. "Because she thinks that I have the soul of a murderer?" He grinned at her, evilly, until she gruffed at him.

"No, it's not that. She ... cheats. She cheats at tiles."

Kanti opened one eye wide. "Oh really? And how does she do that? Can she see through the tiles with gamma rays?"

Tish shrugged. "I don't know how she cheats, but she does. No one can be that lucky."

Kanti rested his head on his paw. "I think you're just being protective. Are you always so protective of your boyfriends?"

Tish growled and flung one of her tiles at him, bouncing it off of his nose. He picked it up from where it had fallen. "Oh, you little stinker. You had the black seven all along!"

Tish stewed a moment longer. "And for your information, I am not protective of my boyfriends!"

"Oh," Kanti said with a grin, "so it's just me then. ..."

Tish snatched the tile back from Kanti and held it in front of his face, menacingly. "You want to see if I can stick this all the way up your nose?"

Kanti put his paws up in surrender and rested back against the couch. Tish lay down on the floor, resting her elbows on the rug. She didn't look up.

"I've never had a girlfriend before," Kanti explained. "So, this is all pretty new territory for me."

Tish looked up at him suspiciously. "How is it possible that you've **never** had a girlfriend?"

Kanti shrugged, self-conscious again. "I don't know. I've asked a few females out, but they've never really been interested. Why? Have you gone out with many males?"

Tish shrugged. "I wouldn't say **many**. I've gone out with a few. I just didn't ... click with any of them."

"Until you started dating me, you mean!" Kanti grinned.

Tish crossed her arms defiantly. "We're not dating."

"What?" Kanti sat up a little straighter, looking a little hurt. "What's that supposed to mean? We're sharing the same apartment ... sharing the same bed. ... How are we 'not dating'?"

"You've never asked me out on a date."

Kanti looked as if he'd been struck across the face. "I haven't?"

Tish shook her head.

With a sudden burst of energy, Kanti leapt to his feet and bolted out the door, slamming it shut behind him. Tish looked up in confusion for a moment before hearing a timid knock at the door.

She stood up to answer it, opening the door only a dozen centimeters. "Yes?"

Kanti stood on the other side, his eyes lowered. "Hey, um, Tish. You might not remember me. I used to work for you at the recycler."

Tish put her paw to her chin and tried to conceal a grin. She pretended to consider him. "Hrm, yes, I *think* I remember you."

Kanti put his paw to the door frame and scratched at an invisible piece of dirt with his thumb claw. "Well, I was thinking ... if you didn't have any plans ... perhaps we ... um, you and I, I mean ... could ... you know ... go out, or something."

"Oh dear, I don't know. This is just so sudden." Tish covered her muzzle with her paw and shook her head. "When were you thinking?"

Kanti stuck his head in the doorway. "How about now?"

"Oh no, no. I couldn't go now. I'm in the middle of a game of tiles," she muttered. "Why, where were you thinking of taking me?"

Kanti smiled and stared into her grey eyes. He took her paw in his. She still held the black seven tile. "Someplace special, Tish. Somewhere I've never taken anyone, ever before."

§

Officer A'hee stepped out of the airlock dragging the middle-aged geroo behind him. With a shove, the fiery red chief of security tossed the pot-bellied male toward Sarsuk's feet. "You wanted to see Doctor Hitera, Commissioner?"

Hitera groveled on his paws and knees, his face pressed against the deck. Sarsuk lowered his head down and sniffed. "Not a particularly impressive specimen," he sighed.

The commissioner tapped his long, curved claws beside the crouching figure, waiting for the doctor to look up. He eventually tired of waiting and flicked him over onto his back. Hitera continued to cower, his trembling paws in front of his face. A strong scent of urine rose from his fur.

"So tell me, Hitera, what is it that the geroo fear more than anything else? Hrm? Doctors know that sort of thing, don't they?" Sarsuk cocked his head. "Every race has something, I suppose, so what is it for geroo?"

The doctor trembled. He sputtered a few sounds, but nothing that could be considered a word.

Sarsuk scooped the geroo up and brought him close to his face. "What about being burned alive, huh? Every race fears fire, right?" The commissioner turned his head to bring one eye closer to the doctor. "Help me out here, can you? Decompression? Suffocation? Drowning!" He blinked. "No?"

"Please! Please don't kill me! I threw myself on the mercy of the court, and they took away ten of my years!" Hitera begged.

Sarsuk ignored his pleas. "Being ripped apart, perhaps? Disemboweled? Oh, I know! What about being eaten alive?"

"Please, please, it wasn't my fault. It wasn't even my idea. I never would have suggested trying to bypass her infertility." Hitera sobbed loudly, his face wet with tears. "It was A'jira! It was all her idea."

The commissioner rested his chin on the heel of his claw a moment, trying to take a measure of his words. "A'jira, you say?"

The doctor rose to his knees. "Yes, it was all her. I was weak. I admit that. She tempted me with her father's credits, and I caved in. But she was the one who actively disobeyed the law. I never even would have considered ..."

"Is she pretty?" Sarsuk's gaping, blue mouth was only a meter away from the cowering geroo. The stench of his breath almost made Hitera gag. "Would you call this A'jira attractive?"

The doctor's head threatened to spin off his shoulders. "P-pretty?" he stammered. "Pretty?" He looked down at the blocky security officer and then back to the commissioner. His heart hammered in his ears. He could hardly hear his own voice. "Well, sure. She's very pretty. Absolutely, yes. She's gorgeous!"

Sarsuk looked over to A'hee, the barest hint of a smile starting to form on the commissioner's amphibious face. The security officer shrugged. "Yeah, I guess so. I saw her in court. She's really young, about my daughter's age. It's kind of hard for me to judge that sort of thing ... without feeling dirty."

Sarsuk nodded and sat back on his haunches after setting the doctor down on the deck. "Excellent! That's great news. Go and fetch her, Officer. Bring her to me."

"Oh thank you, Commissioner!" Hitera said, back to groveling on all fours. "You will not regret this. Thank you so very much!"

"You're quite welcome." Sarsuk returned his attention to his strand and tapped at the screen. "Executing the pretty ones is guaranteed to make an impact. Everyone will be positively glued to their screens," Sarsuk said dismissively.

He flicked his claw in the geroo's direction to indicate their dismissal. "Besides, *two* executions has far more effect on the crew than just the one."

Chapter 30: Ghost Story

Aprisma flipped a tile and grinned. "Red two. Perfect!"

Veni, Arpa, and his mate, Kerra, groaned in unison.

Kerra set her tiles down on the carpet, sitting back in resignation. "We saw the oddest thing on the way here. Security dragged Doctor Hitera off," she said, taking a sip of wine. "He made quite a ruckus while they brought him through the marketplace."

Veni glanced up from his tiles. "Hitera? Is that your doctor, Kerra?"

Kerra's golden eyes blinked from behind a mask of black fur. "No, not mine. He's that doctor from the news a couple of weeks ago."

"Oh, right!" Aprisma lit up. "That scumbag who was cheating the system out of an extra birth token. If you ask me, the court went too easy on him."

Veni gave his mate's round belly a pat. "Yeah, we waited forever for our chance. It'd be totally unfair for rich geroo to line-jump."

"Why they drag him 'way?" Arpa asked, not looking up. "Court no punish him then?"

Veni, Aprisma, and Kerra stared at each other a moment. "Yeah," Aprisma mumbled, "I think he got ten years."

"Perhaps they caught him trying it again?" Kerra wore a concerned expression.

"I don't see how," the other female replied. "They banned him from seeing patients. ..."

"Must'a dun' before." Arpa shrugged, playing a tile beside the others. "Prolly many times 'fore he caught. Prolly gon' try him 'gain in new case."

"But that would mean," Veni whispered, "that we'd be over our bio-limit. No one could be that reckless, could they? What's the point of earning a bunch of credits if you get us all killed? It's not as if you can spend them when you're dead."

Arpa grinned, his white fangs gleamed out of his mass of black fur. "Reminds me. Remember 'Skeleton Crew'? Used to say 'dat story as cub."

Veni nodded but the females just stared at him. "You never heard that story? Through the trinity! We'd always tell that one at sleep-overs when I was a cub. We'd save it until it was really late, and the guys were just barely staying awake."

Aprisma and Kerra shook their heads, staring at him with wide eyes.

"We'd say that the recycler was failing and that it couldn't produce enough oxygen for the entire crew to breathe, but yeah, Arpa, I suppose the same story would work if the ship were over its bio-limit."

Kerra sipped her wine again. "Yeah, so then what happens?"

Veni's ears turned up in an evil grin. He looked like a mischievous child, standing up and dimming the lights. The apartment took on a menacing atmosphere. "After two days of working on the trinity non-stop," he whispered in a spooky voice, "engineering gave up and erected gigantic fans on the agriculture decks to circulate the oxygen generated by the crops.

"But even then, the oxygen levels continued dropping." Veni took a big drink as he sat back down. "Engineering ran the numbers again and again, but the conclusion was clear. Everyone aboard the ship would suffocate unless they could cut the ship's bio-load by seventy-five percent.

"The captain had to make a terrible decision. Oh sure, he could order the least-critical crew members to jump into the recycler. If seventy-five percent did so quickly enough, it would save the lives of the remaining twenty-five percent, but for how long?"

Veni grinned at the females. "You see, even though doing that would save the crew in the short-term, it would doom them all in the long run. Such a reduced gene pool wouldn't be sustainable. Sooner or later, their DNA would grow corrupt from inbreeding, and the entire ship would be lost.

"His only choice ..." Veni explained, "the only *sustainable* choice was to recycle everyone but the breeding age females and enough cubs to eventually replace them – a skeleton crew. The males were reduced to semen samples that would then be used to impregnate the females.

"The females were recycled as soon as they were too old to reproduce. The males were recycled as soon as they were able to produce a semen sample of their own."

"No, 'dat not how it go," Arpa interrupted. "Dey' recycle all male bu' one teenager. He wake up, strap to a gurney, an' hook up a machine. Da machine slowly pumpin' away 'is seed as he make it."

Veni yarped a laugh. "A milking machine? Oh, that's great!"

Aprisma rolled her eyes. "That's silly. There'd be no genetic variety if you only had one male left. That would defeat the whole purpose of a skeleton crew."

"No, Arpa's right. It doesn't have to make sense. It's a ghost story. It just has to be scary," Veni interjected. "And if I heard that version as an adolescent cub, I wouldn't dare fall asleep. I'd be terrified that I'd wake up, strapped to a gurney!"

Veni and Arpa grinned at each other, satisfied by the frightened expressions on Kerra and Aprisma's faces.

"No. ... They can't. ..." Kerra whispered at last.

"I don't want to raise our cub without you." Aprisma held her mate's paw in a death grip.

"It's just a story," Veni whispered, putting a comforting paw to her cheek.

"Is it? Then why did they take semen samples from all the males?"

Chapter 31: Flagged

"Where are you taking me?" Tish asked, starting to sound a little concerned.

Kanti brought her to a dimly lit and mostly deserted portion of deck twenty-four. "We're here," he whispered before unfolding his engineering bag into a vest and putting it on.

Tish's eyes grew wide. "Where did you get that?" she whispered. "You're not supposed to have that. Only the engineering staff is supposed to."

Kanti winked. He turned the handle on an access hatch and pulled it open.

"What are you doing?" she hissed. "You can't do that! You're going to get us in serious trouble."

"Please, Tish, trust me." He kissed her lightly and gestured into the access tube. "Just trust me."

She looked terrified. Tish scanned the hallway again and again, clearly worried that someone saw her.

"Go," he whispered. "No one will see us if we go now."

With worry evident on her face, she finally stepped inside. Kanti followed and closed the hatch behind him. He shone his flashlight on the sensor contacts and showed Tish that they'd been shorted out. "Engineering will never know. From their consoles, it looks as if the hatch was never opened."

"This is a really, really bad idea," she whimpered. "You're going to get us caught. How long have you been doing this?"

Kanti shrugged and took her by the paw. "A few times a week for the past year or so. There's so much to see that I feel as if I won't ever see it all."

"Let's go back, Shaggy. Please?"

Kanti turned to face her. "You don't always do what you're supposed to, do you?"

She shrugged and looked at her boots. "Well, yeah, pretty much."

Kanti sighed. He hated making her unhappy, but he really wanted to share this portion of his life with her. "I know you drink. That's against the ship rules too."

"Everyone drinks," she whispered. "But sneaking around in access tubes is not drinking."

He gave her a little kiss. "Well, perhaps it's high time for you to break a couple more rules. Trust me, please. Just for a bit. This is totally worth it."

Tish hung back for several long minutes as they traversed the maze of access tubes. Kanti held her paw and urged her on. After many years of working in the recycler bay, she wasn't worried about getting dirty, but she feared getting in trouble.

"This is really crazy, Shaggy. You're getting us lost. How could you possibly know which way to go?" she whispered.

Kanti shrugged. "I don't know. I've just always had that sort of memory. Once I see something, I can just always see it again in my mind. I never write anything down."

"Wow, I'd be so lost in seconds here. It's such a maze!"

"Lost is okay," he replied. "It happens sometimes, but there's always a hatch leading out somewhere. The only real risk is forgetting the hatches that are bypassed. If you do that, you could accidentally alert security."

Tish complained less, following along and beginning to show an intense curiosity. "The gravity is so weird in this tube. Why is that?"

"There are a bunch of gravity generators under the commissioner's chambers," Kanti explained. "I think we're feeling bleed-over from that."

Soon, to his surprise and delight, Tish was giggling and urging Kanti forward. She put her arms around him when he came to a stop. She even crawled ahead on one of the long tubes that was too short to stand in.

"This place is incredible. I never would have guessed that all of this was here." She stopped at a heavily insulated door and checked to see whether the sensor was bypassed; it was. "Can we go in this one?"

"No, not that one." He pulled her gently away from the hand-crank. Kanti pointed out the flame and ice crystal icons. "It's far too dangerous in the baffle. Minus thirty-nine degrees according to the gauge. Trust me. You don't want to feel what that's like."

For over an hour, Kanti led Tish all over his favorite haunts. He showed her a wider chamber littered with refuse. "I think some adolescents used to hang out here. There are a few wine bottles tucked away here, but they're all pretty dusty. I don't think they've been back in a long while."

Tish sniffed the air. "Yeah, I think you're right. I don't smell anyone but us."

They walked down a long corridor. "The recycler is really on the other side of this hatch?" She put her paw to the warning icon. "Wow, I guess I just never stopped to wonder how they access it during maintenance."

The pair walked in silence for a long time after, holding paws when they could. Eventually they stopped before an ordinary hatch, and Kanti took a moment to short the sensor closed.

Tish took him by the paws, and he turned to face her. "So … was this one of those secrets you've been keeping from me?" she whispered.

His ears blushed red, and he looked down at their boots. "Yeah," he whispered.

She beamed a smile at him. "You know what? You worried for nothing. I don't hate you."

He wrapped his arms around her. "I love you, Tish. I love you more than I ever thought I could love anyone."

"I love you too," she whispered in his ear.

§

"Shouldn't you be doing something?" Jakari asked.

Ateri smiled at her, ignoring the glass of wine in his paw. He refused to drink while the commissioner was aboard, but he always accepted a glass at parties, so that he could appear sociable. "What do you propose?" he replied in a calm, quiet voice. "Should I loom outside Sarsuk's quarters, waiting for him to summon me? Or select some innocent geroo as scapegoats? Perhaps I should stop random crew members and inspect their birth tokens."

"Very funny," she replied. "I mean like making a contingency plan. Activate the A.I.; select some candidates … just in case he forces us …"

Ateri shook his head.

"Ninety-nine point nine percent of all contingency plans are never needed," she parroted back to him, "and these are likely no different."

"This is different. I refuse to bend on this one. It just goes too far."

Ateri's strand beeped. He took it from his holster and frowned.

"Bad news?" Jakari whispered.

"It could be," he said with a nod. "One of those pages you flagged was just hit."

Jakari's brow wrinkled. "Call security. We can contain this if we act quickly."

Ateri's communicator beeped twice and then three more times in rapid succession. He shook his head. "Let's make our excuses, now. We need to go. It's about to get ugly."

KANTI

Artwork ©2015 Annie Meneses

Chapter 32: Find the Stinker

Kanti closed the hatch behind him.

"Where did we end up?" Tish giggled, still giddy from the adventure. She looked around the wide, clean, and well-lit corridor.

"Saina? Is that you?" a voice called.

Kanti turned to see an old male standing outside an open door with a middle-aged couple. He gestured for the pair to go inside and then hurried over to greet Kanti and Tish.

"You made it! I'm so glad. And straight from work, I see," Charl said, glancing at Kanti's vest. He looked up at Tish, and the old male's eyes sparkled. "And you must be my boy's new love interest! It's such a pleasure to meet you."

"Tish," Kanti said.

"What a lovely name for such a lovely lady! I so look forward to getting to know you."

"Charl," Kanti said to Tish. "My father."

"Your father?" Tish's voice rose in alarm.

"Come right this way," Charl said. "You haven't seen the new place, have you? We only just moved up to deck three a couple of years ago."

Charl ushered the couple inside, and Kanti's mouth hung open in awe. The apartment was absolutely palatial. Enormous original paintings and hand-knotted tapestries hung from cultured marble walls. Party-goers with beautiful jewelry stood about with crystal wine glasses in their paws. Some lounged on leather furniture.

"Tish, you must meet Saina's mother, Marga. Marga, my love, this is Tish, Saina's lady-friend."

"What a pleasure to meet you," Marga said, taking Tish's paw.

Tish turned to face Kanti, confusion and hurt in her eyes. "Your parents?"

Chendra rushed through the crowd and threw her arms around Kanti. "I'm so glad you made it!" She turned to Tish. "I've been dying to meet you. Saina told me all about you! I'm Chendra, Saina's sister."

The muscles in Tish's jaw flexed as she ground her teeth. She stared at Kanti with eyes that could melt steel. "Your family," she growled, raising her voice, "your family that you told me was *dead*?"

Everyone stared now. Kanti's eyes flashed between Tish, Saina's family, and the sea of guests who had all turned in curiosity at the commotion. The live music tapered off.

Tish raised a long arm to point at Chendra. "And Chendra?" Her ears fell back flat against her head. "Your *sister*?"

Tish turned and began to stomp off toward the door, but Kanti grabbed her arm. Teeth flashed, and Tish snarled loudly at him.

"You liar!" she shouted. "You lied to me about *everything*!"

"Wait! Wait!" Kanti pleaded. "I can explain."

Tish grabbed her chest with both paws. Her expression changed from seething anger to the deepest hurt that Kanti had ever seen. This geroo, whom he knew as a pillar of strength, looked as if she'd crumble in on herself at any moment. "You can explain why you lied ... to *me*?"

"No," Kanti said firmly. "I guess I can't explain why, but I can tell you the truth. I owe you that."

Kanti positioned himself between Tish and the door. He held his back straight and tried to project a calmness that he didn't feel. "You mixed us up when we first met, Tish. Saina thought it'd be funny not to correct you, and it seemed harmless enough of a prank, so I played along." He took a deep breath. "I'm sorry – that was cruel.

"I wanted to tell you the truth on a dozen different occasions, but Saina talked me out of it each time. He was my only friend, and I let that cloud my judgment." Kanti wiped a tear from his eye. "After the accident, I went back to you, to set things straight, but it was too late. You'd already reported that I'd been killed."

Tish refused to look at him, so he stepped closer. "I couldn't tell you then. ..."

A silence stretched, so she turned toward him. "Why not? I'd have forgiven you. ..." Her voice was almost inaudible.

Kanti swallowed the lump in his throat. Everyone stared at him. Admitting the truth in public would be beyond foolhardy, but doing anything less would chase Tish away forever. He tried to imagine life without her, his old life alone, hiding in his recycler bay of an apartment. The thought of going back to that was too much to bear.

If only there was some way I could get her alone, he thought.

Suddenly overcome with a weariness that sank in all the way down to his bones, Kanti wondered how much longer he could keep up this charade.

"I don't have a birth token." The words just sort of ... fell out.

The crowd gasped with a single voice. He looked around at the geroo surrounding them. It was too late now for worry. He stared at Tish's wide eyes, her expression unreadable.

"To admit that I was Kanti at that point was committing suicide. I didn't want to lie to you, but I couldn't see any way out of it."

Marga grabbed Kanti by the shoulders, spinning him about. "I knew it!" she shouted. "Where is my boy? Where is my cub?"

Kanti lowered his head. "I'm sorry, Marga. Saina died in the accident. I'm sorry."

Marga swooned to the floor, and several geroo rushed to her side. Kanti tried to step forward, but a powerful paw clamped down on his shoulder. He turned to see a couple with somber, indecipherable expressions. The female was short, white, and curvy. The male was tall, black, and muscular.

His eyepatch was unmistakable.

Ateri escorted Kanti through the crowd and to the door. "I'm sorry, Tish," Kanti shouted over his shoulder. "I'm so sorry. I love you. I will always love you. I hope that you can forgive me someday."

§

Kanti and Ateri walked in silence. Kanti made no effort to escape. "I'm sorry that I lied to you, Captain. I didn't want to. I just didn't have a choice."

Ateri nodded. "I understand. And I'm sorry that I was so hard on you. I thought you were just a formerly rich cub playing some sort of dangerous game."

The two pressed their pads together briefly as they walked – the physical contact signifying that they accepted each other's apologies.

The pair walked in silence a little longer. "You seem very calm," Ateri said suddenly. "You do know where we're headed, right? You're not going to try something stupid, are you?"

Kanti eventually shook his head. "Captain, when you were a cub, did you ever play 'find the stinker'?"

Ateri shrugged. "Sure, who hasn't?"

"My mother told me that I didn't have a birth token when I was only six years old." He took a deep breath and released it slowly. "For the last twenty years, I've been hiding, pretending I'm something that I'm not. It was a very, very long time to hide.

"I'm not relieved that you caught me," Kanti explained, "but I guess I am relieved that it's over. It feels liberating. I feel different than I ever remember feeling before.

"I feel … free."

Chapter 33: Dignity

Ateri walked Kanti to the airlock. Outside the door, a blocky male with a fiery-red pelt leaned against the wall with arms crossed. Beside him, a pot-bellied male sat with his back against the wall, arms wrapped around his legs and forehead resting on his knees. In the middle of the corridor lay a very pretty, young female, her wrists zip-tied behind her back.

The girl screamed and cried. She kicked, she squirmed, she called for her father. Kanti felt relieved when the airlock door finally shut behind him, blocking out most of the racket. Glad that he would be able to meet his fate with his dignity intact, he felt that he'd made the right decision not to try to run.

"Well, this is quite a surprise." Sarsuk said in Krakun. "You've done as I instructed … and I didn't even have to manipulate you! What are you up to now, Ateri?"

Kanti glanced briefly around the chamber. He'd been here once before – in a manner of speaking. He'd seen things and been places that neither the commissioner nor the captain had experienced. He felt energized, with a new sense of self. He had a new life that he wanted back, a desire stronger than any he had felt before.

"Let me guess," the commissioner hissed. "A criminal? Someone already scheduled for execution?" The commissioner lowered his head to get a close look at Kanti.

The tan geroo summoned up all his willpower. He stood with head held high and his paws folded behind his back, mirroring Ateri on Judgment Day. "My name is Kanti. I have no birth token."

Sarsuk glared at Ateri. "You little vermin! You told me that he was dead! What sort of game are you toying at, Ateri?"

"I swapped identities with a friend who was killed," Kanti interrupted. "No one aboard had any way of knowing that the real Kanti was still alive."

Sarsuk stared at the scruffy geroo a long time before scooping him up with his claw. He lifted Kanti far up over the deck, until his claw hovered in front of his face. Kanti steadied himself in the unusual gravity and resumed standing at attention. He did not tremble.

"And so, how is it that you came to be?" Sarsuk studied him with one eye. "How were you born without authorization?"

Kanti glanced down at Ateri. "May we speak in private?"

Commissioner Sarsuk recoiled slightly in surprise before the barest hint of a grin formed on his warty face. "Take the other two down to the recycler, Captain, and wait for us there." He dismissed Ateri with a flick of his free claw.

The captain kept his expression blank. With the smallest of bows, he returned to the airlock and closed the hatch behind him. He was secretly thankful that he was excused, despite Kanti's bold-faced impropriety. He urgently needed to speak with A'hee about the unfolding crisis; Ateri couldn't dare let the commissioner know about it before security at least had a chance the bring the crew back under control.

"What a curious little geroo you are. So bold. I don't think I've ever seen so lowly a crewman face me without fear. I've certainly never seen one dismiss his own captain before." Sarsuk said with a phlegmy chuckle.

"You have that spark. Oh, it's not as bright as Ateri's, certainly, but you have the potential to be something more. Captain, perhaps? Tiny captain." The gargantuan toad grinned wide at his own joke, exposing a terrifying number of meter-long teeth. "It's a shame that you'll be recycled so soon. Ateri has been a source of constant disappointment, you see." Sarsuk's huge face turned dark. "You could have made a fine replacement."

Kanti shook his head carefully. "No, I could never have replaced the captain."

Sarsuk hruffed and let the subject drop. "So tell me, brave, little geroo – how were you conceived?"

Kanti shrugged. "My mother said she didn't know how my father managed to impregnate her. A fluke, I suppose. They just pretended that it'd been an intentional pregnancy, and no one ever questioned it. Why would they?"

"Why, indeed?" Sarsuk chuckled. Krakun body language was notoriously hard for alien races to read, but to Kanti, the commissioner seemed almost disappointed.

"My parents were both recycled years ago." Kanti sighed. "It's too late for you to punish them."

"True enough, but not too late for you, I'm afraid. Your punishment is destined to be … quite an exhibition."

"Punishing me is pointless. I've done nothing wrong." Panic rose in his throat. He pushed it back down. "Well, I've broken rules here and there to keep the truth hidden, but I didn't cheat the system out of a token. I've only played the tiles that I received." Kanti shrugged.

"Yes, yes, punishing you is pointless." Sarsuk nodded. "But it will serve the greater good. What is vitally important is for the rest of the crew to witness how serious a crime it is to breed without authorization.

"Your suffering will be quite extreme. And if they do not wish their ill-gotten offspring to suffer the same fate, then perhaps they'll avoid having them in the first place."

"Lovely." Kanti's ears sagged slightly. "But before you recycle me, may I ask one last question?"

Sarsuk eyed the geroo suspiciously.

"Presuming that I'm the only one, that still means that there have been ten thousand and one geroo aboard the ship during my lifetime, instead of ten thousand. I realize that's not a lot of difference, but wasn't the air supposed to go bad and the trinity supposed to break down? Wasn't the entire ship supposed to come to an end, if we ever exceeded our bio-limit?"

"Yes, I've always found that to be a particularly thin ruse, as well." The commissioner chuckled deep in his gullet. "I'm certain that there must be some limit for the number of geroo who can live aboard a generation ship before the whole system death-spirals, but it certainly wouldn't be as simple as a single number. There would be hundreds of factors."

"So, then why the constant deception?" Kanti asked.

"Because, you simple creature, that's how you control a populace," Sarsuk grunted as if it were obvious. "If I told Ateri that the ship supported ten to twenty thousand geroo, then there'd be twenty thousand on board. And then twenty-one thousand, and then twenty-two …" The commissioner rolled his free claw in the air to show that the process would continue.

"Soon, there really would be a death-spiral; all because the company wasn't controlling what needed to be controlled." He showed Kanti his teeth. "But if I say ten thousand, then ten thousand it will be. If I don't allow flexibility, then it's a little battle once in a while instead a long drawn-out debate over what the ship can and cannot support.

"And I've no interest in debate," he concluded firmly.

"Thank you for leveling with me," Kanti said, nodding. "That's much as I suspected."

Without any warning, Kanti leapt from Sarsuk's claw.

Chapter 34: Eyepatch

"We've got trouble," Ateri said as soon as the airlock door opened.

A'hee nodded. "Crowds are forming on decks seven, nineteen, and twenty-four. I've dispatched security to try to break them up, but I'm not optimistic. Reports say that they're pretty agitated."

"Is anyone organizing this?"

The chief of security shook his fiery mane. "It doesn't appear to be. The crowds started forming a few minutes after a social media explosion. ... Something about a new A.I. the software group just created?"

Ateri cursed under his breath. "We should have vetted the programmer on that project better. Of all the problems we're having right now, that shouldn't be one of them."

"How much force do you want my team to apply?"

The captain shook his head. "Force is liable to make things worse. Have them break up what they can and try to isolate any mob that grows too large." He leaned in close to A'hee and whispered, "Get Hitera and A'jira down to twenty-five. Do it quick, and do it quiet. I don't want the two of them to become catalysts ... or targets."

---------- § ----------

Despite the unusual gravity in the commissioner's chamber, Kanti's aim was good. He struck the plastic hatch cover and shattered it into a dozen pieces, leaving him hanging through the portal on his belly.

"Oof," he groaned, having banged his knee hard on the aluminum wall. He grabbed the ladder rungs with both paws and pulled himself quickly inside.

"What? Get back here!" Sarsuk roared in surprise. With an enormous fist, the commissioner bashed at the open hatchway, smashing the access tube behind it flat.

But Kanti was already sliding down the ladder, his paws and boots gripping the outside rails to slow his descent - no easy task in the chamber's high gravity.

Kanti hit the ground hard and began scuttling across the chamber's sub-flooring at top speed. "Stop! Stop him! Ateri!" screamed Commissioner Sarsuk. "He's fled into the access tubes! Apprehend him!"

Kanti spun open the hand-wheel that sealed the airlock and rolled inside. He cycled the chamber and then unsealed the heavily insulated doorway to the bulkhead baffle, without actually opening the hatch. Only then could he relax.

All airlocks were designed so that one hatch cannot be unsealed before the opposite hatch has been closed and locked. No geroo could pursue from the chamber directly behind him.

§

"Do something, now!" Sarsuk shouted.

Ateri felt as if his teeth would rattle out of his head. He pressed one ear shut with his paw in a feeble attempt to filter the commissioner out. Meanwhile, he shouted orders into his strand to the duty officer, trying to be heard over the roar. "I want eyes on all the access hatch sensors! Find out where he's headed, and relay the coordinates to security! I need security officers positioned at any hatch he might be headed toward!"

He turned to Sarsuk. "I'm on it!" Ateri shouted as soon as the commissioner paused for a breath. The captain spun the hand-wheel to the airlock and stepped back inside. He took a deep breath and gave thanks for the relative quiet inside the airlock as the air cycled.

§

Kanti quickly arranged all of the items he'd need. Although he still lacked an air monitor, he was thankful that Saina's funds allowed him to buy so many common items that he'd denied himself previously.

He started by unfolding a silvered, polyester film, emergency blanket. He wrapped it around his body and tied the ends in front of his chest, leaving him looking like a gigantic, fuzzy sandwich wrapped in aluminum foil. Then he put on the anti-fog safety goggles to trap the warm air in front of his eyes. He wrapped a heavy bandana around his head to protect his ears and help keep his head warm. He mounted his flashlight to the safety goggles and put on the silicone gloves.

Kanti still had nothing to warm the air that he breathed in. He'd considered packing a cigar in his kit with the hopes that it'd help, but he'd eventually decided against it. Not being a smoker, Kanti thought it might end up causing more problems than it attempted to solve. Regardless, he was confident that he was far better prepared to enter the baffle with his new setup than he had been originally.

Kanti gripped the hand-wheel on the hatch and steadied his nerves. The indicator read -40C. His blood ran cold even as he thought about it.

The strand on his shoulder beeped once.

"Kanti? Can you hear me?" It was Ateri's voice.

Kanti held his breath, afraid to even move. He figured that the captain must have used his broadcast privileges to send to his communicator without waiting for him to pick up. He froze, unsure of what to do. Should he reply? Ignore it? He considered answering, but he already had the heavy gloves on, and he would probably have to untie the emergency blanket just to reach his shoulder.

"If you can hear me, just listen." It sounded like an airlock cycling in the background. The captain whispered to keep his voice down. "I know you're scared and that you want to run. I'd be scared, too."

Hearing the captain's voice chilled Kanti. He thought about how good it felt to swallow his fear. He had talked to Sarsuk as if he were the commissioner's equal. The enormous creature had seen it in him — Kanti's potential to be more. He hadn't begged. He didn't run. ... Until now.

He remembered the pretty girl in the corridor with her hands tied behind her back — and how superior he had felt at the time.

"But I want you to think this through. You're a bright guy. There's no way off the ship. Even if you manage to hide, you can't stay hidden for long. You're only prolonging this. ... Playing 'find the stinker' again."

Ateri took a deep breath. Kanti's paws trembled, but still he said nothing.

"You don't know what the commissioner's like," the captain confessed. "I've never seen him this angry. There's no guessing what he might do, or who he might hurt.

"Call me back at this number, please. Turn yourself into me. I'm headed over to sick bay now. I'm sure they'll have something that you can use to block the pain. You won't have to go out suffering. But I can't get it to you if you don't turn yourself in."

Kanti's mind spun. Perhaps the captain was right. Maybe giving up wasn't "quitting." Maybe it was the right thing to do.

The airlock finished cycling, and now Kanti heard only the sound of Ateri's shallow breaths. "I have to go now.

Think about what I said, and think quickly. Think about the skeleton crew. Please don't let that happen."

With a click, the connection severed.

"Skeleton crew?" Kanti mouthed silently. *Surely the commissioner wouldn't do that. Would he? He couldn't. Besides, he'd need a semen sample ... from ... every ...*

Kanti's heart pounded in his ears. The commissioner already had samples from all the male crew members. The crew had been tricked! Sarsuk had been preparing to recycle almost everyone. He'd been planning it since his last visit, and now that he was ready, he had returned to the White Flower II early, to conduct mass murder.

Kanti stumbled backwards slightly, feeling dizzy.

After a moment of regaining his nerves, Kanti shook his head. *It couldn't be that. I'm just being paranoid!*

Kanti threw the hatch open and climbed quickly down the three stories of handholds. It was cold, certainly; the air burned his nose and lungs, but he knew where he was going, and he was prepared. By the time he emerged from the second airlock, he wasn't even shivering. He quickly discarded his cold-weather gear and hurried down the corridor with flashlight in paw.

———— § ————

Ateri emerged from the airlock to find himself surrounded by a mob of geroo.

"There he is!" a voice shouted. "Grab him!"

A hundred paws smothered him, grabbing fistfuls of his fur, ripping the fur from its roots. They twisted his arms, cruelly, behind his back.

The crowd rushed away leaving the corridor empty and silent.

On the deck, forgotten, laid a trampled eyepatch.

Chapter 35: Salvage

The crowd poured into the market area. Ateri cried out in pain as they passed him roughly overhead, dumping him unceremoniously onto the dais normally reserved for performers. A rioter threw a length of power cable up over the scaffolding that held the spotlights for the stage. A crude loop in the cable's end hung down one short step off the edge of the dais.

"Stop!" Jakari screamed at the top of her lungs.

The din tapered and then the crowd fell silent. A space opened up around the captain's mate, and she rushed to the stage, pushing her way roughly through the crowd and up onto the dais on which Ateri was held.

She turned to the crowd and shouted, "The captain isn't the enemy! Listen to him! Let him explain."

All eyes moved from Jakari to Ateri, and a few voices grumbled. The mob shifted suddenly, shoving Ateri to the edge of the dais. His toes hung just off the edge of the stage, his battered face positioned just behind the loop of power cable.

Ateri's black fur was blood-slicked. He'd lost a front incisor, and without the eyepatch, the left side of his face looked sunken and malformed.

"I am not your enemy," he announced in a calm and commanding tone. "You have no enemies aboard this ship."

"We're over our bio-limit!" a face in the crowd shouted. "You were going to recycle us down to a skeleton crew!"

All eyes focused on the captain. His broken, left arm hung uselessly at his side; his right ear was in tatters.

Ateri made an effort to stand up straight. "We may be over our bio-limit. I doubt it, but Commissioner Sarsuk certainly believes so."

The crowd gasped in shock and horror. A dozen different rioters jockeyed their strands above the sea to get clear footage of the captain. The images streamed live to every deck.

"Will he order us to recycle some of the crew to restore the balance?" Ateri asked. "I have no way of knowing that. If he does, I will argue it. But I will be honest with you – I doubt that I will be able to sway him."

The mob buzzed with a thousand voices. "You created an A.I. to decide who lives and who gets recycled!"

Ateri nodded and grimaced in pain. "Yes, we did. And if we ever have to use that artificial intelligence, we'll switch it off as soon it generates the lists. No one – not even the A.I. – will have to live with the guilt of making those hard decisions."

The crowd buzzed again. Scattered shouts and screams rang out, but no one voice stood out over the others.

"Sacrifice is an essential component of life," Ateri shouted to the crowd. "We all make sacrifices. We go without the things that we **want**, so that our cubs can have the things that they **need**. We work late hours, when we must. We sacrifice our leisure at times to keep this ship running.

"We live in a time of peace, but before the Exodus, our young geroo fought wars. They marched off to battle, knowing that they might be sacrificing themselves to protect their friends and families."

With his good arm, Ateri wiped at the blood dripping from his nose. "Will some of us have to make that same sacrifice to ensure the survival of the rest? I don't know the answer to that question.

"But if it comes to that, I know that we will." Ateri surveyed the crowd with his remaining eye. "Of that, I have no doubt."

§

His strand beeped again. "Attention, tiny captain," the voice said in Krakun.

Kanti froze. "Tiny captain?" he mouthed. He pulled the device off his shoulder and stared at the close-up image of Commissioner Sarsuk giving a ship-wide broadcast.

"I am very disappointed in this new turn of events," the commissioner explained. "I am a very busy krakun. I have things to do and places to be. Cleaning up this mess puts me behind schedule.

"In precisely half an hour, you can find me in the recycler bay – executing geroo. And I will continue executing geroo until you get your turn. But I suspect that if you ask nicely, you can push your way to the front of the line."

Kanti slumped in disbelief against the wall of the access tube.

"If you wish to continue hiding, you go right ahead. I will find you," the commissioner explained. "You see, eventually so few geroo will be left on board that not enough will remain to maintain the trinity. It will shut down, and the ship will grow very, very cold.

"But don't worry about me. I'll reroute one of the other generation ships to come out and rendezvous with the

White Flower II. They'll be here in … oh, a decade or two, to salvage the ship and the ten thousand birth tokens your crew will leave behind.

"I will find you … when some geroo complains about the smell emanating from your final hiding place."

Kanti sank slowly to the floor, feeling utterly defeated.

"Oh, and one last thing," the commissioner added. "To encourage you to hurry, I'm going to put all of your friends, your coworkers, and everyone else that I think you might care about up at the front of the line."

Chapter 36: Recycled

Precisely half an hour had passed since the last ship-wide broadcast. Strands ship-wide beeped once more, and thousands of wide, unblinking eyes stared at the displays.

"Crew of the White Flower II," the commissioner's image announced in krakun, "you've been betrayed by one of your own doctors." The enormous amphibian's horizontally slit eyes turned down for a moment while he plucked a screaming Hitera up by the leg.

"Please, you must believe me! It wasn't my fault!" the portly, little geroo begged.

"You entrusted him with the responsibility for keeping you healthy, and what has he done?" Sarsuk sniffed briefly at the squirming creature that he dangled high above the recycler belt. "He has conspired to violate the most sacred rule that we krakun have given the geroo when we hired you to operate this ship! You must not exceed a bio-limit of six hundred thousand crew·years."

"I wasn't going to do it!" the doctor screamed. "Please!"

"What will happen if you exceed the ship's bio-limit?" Commissioner Sarsuk boomed.

The view turned to show a long line of geroo leading out of the recycler bay. Several stared up in horror at the atrocity unfolding above them. Most others kept their eyes down at their paws or shut tightly as they held one another.

"Your recklessness will spell the death of all these geroo!"

Finding the execution queue wasn't difficult. It stretched out of the recycler bay doors, down the corridor, and off into the distance. The cacophony of so many screaming geroo was deafening. Some comforted and reassured others, some nursed their cubs, the wrists of a few were even bound to keep them from struggling. Grim security officers stood watch at even intervals.

Kanti ran past the blur of faces. Many, too worried about their own fates, did not appear to notice him, but some recognized that he had to be the "tiny captain" to whom the commissioner was broadcasting. They rejoiced. They urged him to hurry. They fell to their knees in prayer.

Kanti rounded the corner, nearly out of breath. He recognized a few faces here and there in the queue – the florist, the dirembo player, the captain's mate – but here in the recycler bay stood everyone that he knew and cared for: Chendra, Charl, Marga, Arpa, Kerra and her cubs, Veni, Aprisma, and of course, Tish.

Sarsuk loomed over the conveyor belt. He turned his enormous head to face Kanti in the doorway. Dr. Hitera's remains lay on the belt, making their long, slow journey into the violet light. In the commissioner's claws was A'jira, with paws still bound and long, bloody loops of intestine hanging down from her open belly.

"So, you made it at last," Commissioner Sarsuk sneered.

Kanti rested his paws on his knees, doubled over and struggling to catch his breath. He thought of Saina trying to catch his breath at almost precisely the same spot on the blue deck and smiled, momentarily savoring the happy memory. "I came ... as fast ... as I could," Kanti managed as he panted.

Sarsuk dropped the pretty, young female's remains as if she were a forgotten doll.

"I'm here. I'm here. Go home, all of you, please," Kanti said to the long line of geroo.

"You don't give the orders here, tiny captain!" Sarsuk snapped in Krakun.

"You wanted the crew to fear what would happen if they disobeyed you, and they do." Kanti took a moment to catch his breath. He stood tall and controlled his trembling. "Now you can show them that *obeying* your orders will be rewarded with mercy."

The two stared unblinking into each other's eyes. No one made a sound.

"Very well," Sarsuk finally croaked. "The rest of you can go."

The masses shared a deep breath of relief. Kanti so wanted to go to Tish, or even to turn to make sure that she was okay, but he wasn't ready to take his eyes from the krakun.

In moments, the noise of rapidly departing geroo faded behind him. Kanti folded his paws behind his back.

Sarsuk put out his enormous claw. Blood and gore dripped from his stony talons. "And now, tiny captain, it's your turn."

Captain Ateri, filming the broadcast with his strand, turned to face Kanti. His left arm hung in a sling made from a length of power cable.

But instead of walking straight to the commissioner, Kanti walked to the side, circling around the blue deck. "You're the one in a hurry, but I'm in no rush," he explained. "Come and get me."

Sarsuk growled slightly before charging at the scruffy geroo. Kanti gasped in shock at just how quickly the behemoth could move.

At the last possible moment, Kanti sprinted away. The commissioner's enormous claw closed on empty air. Kanti was glad that Sarsuk wasn't under his native gravity, or the tan geroo might not have been so lucky.

"Surely you can do better than that!" Kanti shouted.

Sarsuk growled in frustration and took a deep breath. Krakun were astounding creatures. They could weather the most punishing, alien environments with only minor discomfort. Had a geroo breathed in so much Krakuntec air, his lungs would blister. "I will make you wish that you'd never been born!" he roared.

The commissioner's claw swatted down on the deck. Kanti rolled out of the way and barely managed to duck beneath the creature's huge tail as it swept the deck.

"Do be careful, now!" Kanti laughed. "You won't be able to make me suffer, if I'm crushed flat."

Sarsuk wiped away the crustiness forming in the corners of his eyes. "You'd better hope that the medics cannot revive you," he growled. "For if they can, I will make sure that your death stretches longer than any ..."

Sarsuk dove at the tiny geroo with arm outstretched.

With a running leap, Kanti dove too – through the massive archway and directly into the violet light.

The commissioner froze in place for a long moment as he realized what had happened.

He screamed so loud that the decks themselves rumbled. Sarsuk pulled his arm out of the recycler, and clenched his remaining claw around the stump, desperately trying to stem the flow of blood that coursed out of it.

Captain Ateri turned his strand around so that it no longer recorded the scene. The expression on his battered face was calm and business-like. "All crew members with quick access to the following items must bring them immediately to Recycler Bay Two: ratchet straps, ropes, fire hoses, pry-bars – anything that can be used to fashion an enormous tourniquet."

Ateri looked up for a moment to survey the commotion beyond the camera's eye. Sarsuk's screaming in the background could not be ignored. "Crew members with access to blowtorches, welders, or anything that could be used to cauterize a wound will do the same. Medics," Ateri twitched a shredded ear, momentarily unsure of what he could instruct them to do, "bring anything that could assist with a traumatic amputation - anything and as much as you can carry."

§

Ateri held a trembling Jakari with his right arm. "I was so scared," she whispered, ignoring the sea of chaos that surrounded them. First responders rushed toward the recycler while other crew members rushed away. "I've never been so scared."

He shushed her. "I had great faith in Kanti. I knew that he'd come through. Just as I was certain that the crew would do the right things."

"You knew?" Her eyes filled with tears. "How could you possibly be so sure?"

Ateri stared at her beautiful face for a long while before pushing his lips up against her ear. He spoke so quietly that even she had difficulty hearing him amid all the noise and confusion. "Truthfully, I did think that I might lose you," he whispered. "I've never been so frightened in my whole life."

They held each other gently, enjoying the moment and ignoring the rest of the crew. The other geroo rushed by, paying them no notice either.

At last, Jakari giggled, giddy with the sudden turn of events.

"Something's funny?" Ateri asked. "Because I could really use a laugh right now."

"Well, the next time that damned recycler acts up, at least we'll know one thing for certain," she said.

"Oh yeah, what's that?" he asked with a smile that highlighted his missing tooth.

Jakari pressed her lips against his ear this time. "Well, no matter the issue, we'll know for a fact that Sarsuk had a hand in it."

Chapter 37: Honor

Captain Ateri addressed the crew of the White Flower II once more, but this time from the bridge. His fur was clean and brushed. His mended left arm hung in a cloth sling. "I want to personally thank the crew," he said, "for pulling together during these last few hours. This cycle's events were without precedent, but as always, your efficiency and professionalism have been unequaled.

"The commissioner has been stabilized after his injury. He's now headed back to Krakuntec, where he can get medical care from his own physicians. Our medics on board assure me that krakun doctors will be able to graft on a new claw and forearm, once they clone a replacement. Meanwhile, Commissioner Sarsuk will be laid up for several weeks, at least."

Ateri cleared his throat. "I do not know, at this point, whether the company will send another commissioner to supervise our progress, or if we will simply operate without any direct oversight during the interim. Either way, I know that I can count on all of you to continue to do your jobs as expertly as you've always done, throughout this mission."

The captain rubbed his chin for a moment, lost in thought. "Many of you out there had the pleasure of knowing Kanti before this incident at the recycler. For those of you who weren't fortunate enough to have met this brave, young geroo, I wanted to share a few words on his passing.

The commissioner wanted to make an example of Kanti, to remind us all of how important it is that we never exceed the ship's bio-limit.

"But what I saw here, this cycle, was a sterling example of self-sacrifice for the greater good. Kanti gave of himself to save all of us.

"Some of you said that this crisis was his fault in the first place. That his very existence and his reactions were what brought us to the precipice. To them I say that I hope they are never judged by circumstances beyond their control. I hope that they are never forced into a similarly dire situation."

From the corridor outside of her lab, Chendra wiped away her tears. Charl and Marga begged her to stay with them, but she needed to be alone with her thoughts. She hoped that it might be easier to work through the pain, rather than share it with others.

She felt angry at Kanti's deception, of course, but then again, Chendra had grown closer to him than she'd ever been to her actual brother. Looking back, she wondered if she'd ever really known Saina at all. She hated to admit that her treasured memories of him, growing up, were only an admiration for what her big brother represented. She wondered how her feelings for Kanti had colored those memories.

She hesitated outside the door to the laboratory as she watched Ateri's broadcast on her strand. But now that she was here, she was no longer certain that she could get any work done. So many memories of the time she had shared with Kanti came flooding back.

She wondered if she should seek out Kanti's girlfriend; if getting to know her might make things better or worse. Tish must be feeling much the same sorts of conflicting emotions as Chendra was. She nodded to herself. Even if meeting her did turn out to be awkward and weird, it would be worth the risk.

The broadcast from the bridge continued. "And for that reason, I am pleased to declare Kanti a hero of the geroo," Ateri announced. "In honor of his passing, the trinity will be shut down for a full cycle of mourning."

Chendra's eyes popped open. "A shutdown?"

Chendra ran into the lab and over to her lab bench. "No, not yet, not yet!" she muttered as she fumbled for where she had left her gear. "Please let me get into position first!"

Chendra reached out for her quantum resonator and froze in place just as her outstretched paw was about to grasp the black rectangle. The inset screen was lit with an image of Captain Ateri giving his ship-wide broadcast.

"It is true that he lived with a borrowed birth token, even though he hadn't been born with it," the tiny image of Ateri said. "That token and the token belonging to A'jira have now been passed along to their rightful owners – a new pair of Happy Couples. But in honor of what Kanti has done here for us today, I am posthumously assigning him the token that had belonged to the criminal, Hitera.

"And when we pass that token on to a new Happy Couple, later tonight we will consider it to have been Kanti's all along, instead of belonging to its original owner. In this way, we will honor his memory and the legacy of the sacrifice that he has made for us all."

"What's this?" Chendra muttered, picking up the strand. The quantum resonator didn't contain any real communication components. It couldn't even power the display, much less play a live feed. She turned the device over and stared at the deep scratches in its case.

§

Tish trudged down the corridor, ignoring the revelers, the drinkers, and the dancers. She ignored the loud, happy voices on all sides. She wanted nothing more than to be alone, to bury her muzzle in a book, or perhaps watch a cheerful musical.

Tish slumped against her apartment door, emotionally exhausted. She tried to lift her paw to her communicator to punch in her code, but it refused to obey.

There on the deck, in front of the door, lay a small tile, with a black seven printed on its face. She scooped the tile up and clutched it tightly to her chest.

"Bad day, huh?" a friendly voice whispered behind her.

Tish froze. She turned around so slowly that it looked as if she had barely moved at all. Her heart hammered in her chest.

"But, but, you died," she whispered softly. "I saw you get recycled with my own eyes. Everyone thinks you're dead."

Kanti was filthier than she'd ever seen him. He looked used-up and spent.

"That happens to me … sometimes … it seems." His laugh wasn't so much mirthless as it was very tired.

She reached a trembling paw to him. His chest was warm to the touch.

"What are you doing here?" she whispered. "Someone will see you. Why didn't you let yourself in?"

"I wasn't certain that I'd still be welcome. Besides –" He took the quantum resonator out of the holster on his shoulder, "– I seem to have misplaced my strand."

The hard lines on her forehead began to soften. "But … how?" she whispered.

"I borrowed it from Chendra's lab after I escaped from Sarsuk," Kanti gestured with the device. "She thought it might shut the trinity down."

"Might?"

"It was better odds than if I didn't try it." Kanti shrugged. "I didn't actually expect it to work. When I jumped through, I really thought that would be the end. When it wasn't. … Well, I was so shocked that I nearly fell right on my tail.

"But the violet light disappeared, and I found myself on the other side of that hatch we saw on our date. I made it through just before the commissioner could grab me.

"Bad luck for him. I guess the trinity turned back on again as soon as the quantum resonator was outside the chamber."

Tish stared at him in disbelief, unblinking, her muzzle slightly open.

"So, I was thinking," he whispered, "that if you weren't all that angry at me. … Perhaps we could go out some time?"

Tish wrapped her arms around him, and the pair collapsed to the deck.

They cried. They laughed. They shook uncontrollably. They kissed.

"So. … Tiny captain?" she whispered at last.

Kanti shrugged. "It's not the worst possible nickname, I suppose." He kissed her once more. "But you can call me 'Shaggy'."

Her powerful arms squeezed him so tightly that he found it hard to take a breath. "Please, please tell me you don't have any more secrets," she begged.

Kanti chuckled. "I have lots of secrets," he whispered. "But they're all just things that I haven't told you yet."

The End

Artwork ©2015 Cunningfox

Thank you so much for reading *Skeleton Crew*!

Have you got a moment? Please leave a review on my Amazon listing (http://www.amazon.com/dp/B00MKCJSQI) or drop me a quick e-mail (gre7g.luterman@gmail.com) and let me know what you thought of the tale.

I really appreciate it! Feedback of any kind helps keep the creative juices flowing and makes me want to write more.

Epilogue: One Year Later

by Rick Griffin

"I absolutely promise, out of here by dinner. Topside with a rocket in my tail, Chendra and the folks already have – yes, I'm good for it! There's a reason that –"

Behind him, the captain cleared his throat. In a single motion, Kanti jumped, turned out of his chair, and saluted.

"Personal calls on your first day, junior officer?" Ateri asked. He stood rigidly with his chest out, hands clasped behind his back.

Six hundred excuses paraded themselves through Kanti's mind in high speed video. He considered each in turn; his eyes twitched one way, the corner of his mouth another.

It was stupid. His shoulders slumped. "My deepest apologies, captain."

"I remember my first time in the academy," Ateri said, stepping around Kanti. With one finger he flipped through the files on the desk's screen. "Always with the video chat in the corner of my screen, flirting with the third-shift girls. Up all night drinking with the guys when we should have been doing homework. Wrote a program once that let me cheat on the officer's test, which itself ended up impressing the professor."

"Really?" Kanti asked, eyes wide.

"No, not really." Ateri stared with his good eye. "I was a model student. You don't get to be captain if they catch you always running around causing trouble."

With his other hand, Ateri pulled out the engineering vest that he was holding. He dropped it on Kanti's seat. Kanti bared his teeth sheepishly.

"You may be a hero," Ateri said, "but you're not an engineer yet."

"Captain ..." Kanti sighed deeply. He didn't know how to say what he wanted without further offense.

Ateri didn't appear perturbed, but he rarely did. "Yes?"

"What do you do when the pressure gets too much for you?"

Ateri furrowed his brow. "The pressure is always too much. You learn to tread water."

"But what about the times you feel like you're about to explode?"

"At that point," Ateri said, "I go home and sleep with my mate. You have one of those, as I understand."

"Yes sir."

"Oh little captain!" Tish's voice blurted from Kanti's phone.

Kanti nervously grinned again and pulled the phone back up to his face. "In a moment, love. I'll see you after my shift."

Tish winked. "Maybe we can invite the captain and his mate to dinner sometime."

"I don't think –"

"That sounds lovely, actually," Ateri interjected. "Do you have Jakari's number?"

"I'll pick it up from the officer registry. Don't work too hard!" The video cut out.

Kanti pushed the phone back into its holder on his shoulder. "Am I in trouble?"

"Not if that dinner is any good," Ateri said. He pointed to the screen on the desk. "However, right now it appears you're wanted to observe the compressor replacement on deck nineteen. Live experience is always better than simulated. Don't miss it."

"Yes captain!"

Kanti saluted. Ateri saluted back. Kanti turned to go, but Ateri raised a finger.

"One more thing," Ateri said, "That nickname. The crew keeps calling you 'little captain'."

"I have noticed that, sir."

"Where did that come from?"

Kanti held up his hands. "By my birth token sir, I have no idea."

Kanti passed through the doors out of the room. Ateri looked briefly at the manifest on his phone. Then, his ears twisted up, and he turned his head toward the empty doorway.

He smirked.

31806745R00149

Made in the USA
San Bernardino, CA
20 March 2016